MW00943473

THE PREACHER'S PROMISE

A HOME TO MILFORD COLLEGE NOVEL

BY PIPER HUGULEY

Liliaceae Press

Copyright © 2014. Liliaceae Press.

Cover by JShan

Editors: Sally Bradley and Stacye Anderson

This book is licensed for your personal enjoyment only. This book may not be re-sold or given away to other people. If you would like to share this book with another person, please purchase an additional copy for each person. If you're reading this book and did not purchase it, or it was not purchased for your use only, then please return it and purchase your own copy. Thank you for respecting the hard work of this author. To obtain permission to excerpt portions of the text, please contact the author at huguleyriggins@hotmail.com

All characters in this book are fiction and figments of the author's imagination.

For Dad. I forgot to get you a birthday present last year when we were learning about Mom. So, this one is for you.
Happy Birthday.
I love you.

CHAPTER ONE

Oberlin, Ohio- 1866

Amanda Stewart had nothing but the clothes on her back.

Ladies were not allowed to take Tabulation courses at Oberlin College, but she understood the red underlines at the end of the column of figures.

She needed to ask anyway.

"There's nothing?" Her Leghorn bonnet made it a little more difficult to lift her head, but she had to get a clearer view of her father's law partner, Mr. Henry.

And she instantly regretted looking to him. Slimy Charles Henry made his way around to her side of his desk, to provide an intimate explanation to her, a newly impoverished daughter of Ham, just what it all meant for her.

The weakness in her stomach brought across her new reality plainly enough, and she clenched the folds of her crisp bombazine black mourning dress into her wet palms. At least gripping the material would dry her sweaty palms and give her wrists some strength. She needed strength now. *Help me through this, God.*

Reduced now to this new status—that of a poor russet-brown colored woman with a brand new college degree,--she adjusted the new bonnet but the gesture provided no comfort. She would have to endure the moist explanations of Mr. Henry straight into her delicately coiled ear, just above the tourmaline earbobs that her father had given her last birthday.

"Miss Stewart, your father was an abolitionist who saw to it that every penny that he had went to ending slavery. And he succeeded. That evil has been removed from the face of the earth in keeping with God's holy principle of thou shalt earn thy own bread from thine own sweat."

He sat up from his explanations and she bit the inside of her cheek to keep from laughing. Mr. Henry pulled out a handkerchief that had seen better days and mopped down his pink brow with it. The yellowing handkerchief made a trip around Mr. Henry's rather round and bulbous head soaking up all of the excess moisture on his face, head, and neck. By the time the cloth emerged, it was brown. Her desire to laugh decreased immediately.

"Yes, Father's cause has won the day. But he always saw to me and made sure that I was comfortable."

"Lawrence Stewart loved you much, child. He made sure you had the finest clothes, books, lessons to play the piano, deportment, and the, well, craziest idea of you taking the college course at Oberlin. Well, my goodness, that was certainly a waste of his money wasn't it?"

His recounting of how much her father loved her, combined with his recent passing a few weeks ago and now this horrible situation of her impoverishment caused her to bring out her own embroidered handkerchief.

His insult only hit her after she had wiped at the small tears at the corners of her eyes.

"Mr. Henry, my father was not just a fighter for slavery but an ardent believer in the strong hearts, minds, and bodies of women.

He saw to it that my mother had her own education before he married her. When my mother died, he vowed he would do the same thing for me." Amanda pocketed the handkerchief again since the desire to cry went away as she addressed his slight to her intelligence.

"Oh my," Mr. Henry slid himself around and sat on the corner of his desk, facing her. His posture was most inappropriate, but propriety for her feelings didn't matter, now that she was defenseless and poor. His shift in bringing his oily person closer to hers made her heart pound hard beneath the high collar of her bombazine. "I surely did not mean to offend, Miss Amanda, I did not. I just wanted you to know of my concern for your present situation."

She fixed him with a gaze. "I appreciate your concern, but I only wanted what rightfully belonged to my father out of this practice. My Oberlin education has not afforded me the luxury of being a lawyer."

His blue eyes blinked in surprise at her. "Oh, ho. Miss Amanda. A lawyer? What??" And he backed off from her, wiping his eyes and bending over double in laughter at the preposterous thought.

She sat in the chair stiff, watching her father's law partner amuse himself at her expense, all of the while calculating, turning over in her mind what she had, and what she could keep. She had some other dresses that could be sold and that might be enough to live on for a while. It was a mere turn of a phrase for her to be a lawyer, of course, but what could she do with her new Oberlin degree? She didn't want to nurse. The smell of blood made her faint. And nurses had to deal with unwashed bodies. It was enough to deal with Mr. Henry's less than fastidious grooming at this point.

Mr. Henry straightened up and wiped at his eyes with his soggy brown handkerchief. "Yes, well. What to do, what to do? Lawrence had no other family and neither did your poor mamma. Are there any young men on the horizon? Marriage, perhaps?"

"Marriage?" She nearly hooted out the heinous word, but that was not proper behavior.

Her stomach would have turned over and plunged to her shoes if her stomach weren't already there at the limited prospects of her new life

"Yes, someone over to the college you've been attending class with. I mean, while you attended the Ladies' course."

"I attended a Gentleman's course or two."

"You did? Oh my. Well, no matter that. Any possible candidates?"

"No." Even if there were, she wasn't sure she should tell him.

Mr. Henry arranged himself behind his desk. "Well, that's too bad. A properly educated dusky maiden such as yourself should be taken proper care of. By someone."

The look in his eyes shifted in a way that Amanda did not care for. At all. His blue eyes narrowed and fixed themselves on the rounded shape of her bombazine basque.

Every drop of blood in her body plummeted to her toes and she stood up, so that the blood would somehow shoot back up to the rest of her body against gravity. She must cease this regard her father's law partner had for her person. "I am not interested in marriage. And since I'm a Christian woman, the only arrangement I could be interested in would be marriage. I may have a brown skin tone, Mr. Henry, but I will be no man's soiled dove."

The smirk on his features quickly departed. "Yes. Well. Marriage would be the only thing for you."

"I couldn't marry for anything other than love, Mr. Henry."

He spread his hands and she had never noticed before how well groomed Mr. Henry's hands were. For a man. Although her father had been a lawyer, his hands looked like that of a working man's until the day he died nearly two weeks ago. "An idealistic point of view in such a cold, cruel world. I pray you find the love you seek, but it will be difficult for one like you."

She moved her dress from beneath the desk and edged out to the door. "Good day to you, Mr. Henry."

"Good Day, Miss Amanda Stewart. Your father was a special man and he will be sorely missed. I wish you, the only offspring he had, the best of lives."

Before she knew it, she was on the other side of the door, outside in the spring air, knowing Charles Henry for a liar.

She had no evidence of his untruths. But the shaky feeling in the marrow of her bones set off all kinds of alarms within her that shot up and down her arms and legs, leaving her cold in the warm May air. He had not told her the full story.

She walked along Front Street of Oberlin back to the small house they had rented and spent the next hour pawing through her father's papers for some evidence. There must be some scrap of something to condemn Charles Henry with.

Nothing.

But the last envelope she grasped was a letter that came for him after his death.

Dear Lawrence Stewart,

We have heard much of your career in spreading the epistle of education among the Negro people. And in that cause, we would like to engage you to come to Milford, Georgia to the Milford plantation to teach the recently freed slaves reading and writing skills. Given the strength of your purpose, we have enclosed a train ticket for you to come. Please wire ahead to let us know of your arrival. Signed, Mayor Virgil Smithson.

Amanda clutched at the envelope. *Thank you, God.* She now had a purpose. The Missionary Society had come around to various classes at Oberlin all the time to solicit teachers of the race to go South to teach their newly freed brethren the skills in literacy. She had paid them no mind, because she did not need to. Then. And as for her father, didn't these people know that her father was a lawyer and not a teacher?

No matter, because as many times as she closed her mind to the opportunity before, this seemed to be the answer to her predicament now. The Missionary Society did not promise much money, but it was better than nothing and included a home to stay in and meals. She would sell off what she could of the books, but keep certain ones to send to the new school, as well as his diaries, which would be a comfort to her.

God's hand was in this. And in His mercy, He guided her gently away from the prospect of a horribly disgraced life to one encompassing pride and dignity. She rose on stiff knees and arched her aching back to send a wire to Mayor Smithson right away, lest he find someone else to take up the engagement.

Her father would be so proud of her—taking up the task of teaching their recently freed brethren how to read and write. Certainly a worthy work to take up in the name of God.

And, in the heat of Georgia, she would find out out some way to figure out just what Charles Henry was hiding from her.

"We late to pick up the teacher, Papa."

Virgil Smithson looked down into the bright black button eyes of his daughter and patted her on the shoulder. "I see, honey.

Had some extra customers to the shop. Couldn't be helped. The new teacher will wait on the platform."

March had put on her best dress, a white hand-me-down from one of the Milford grandchildren, which was too short. March tugged on it again, and her little spindly brown legs arched out from under the dress in a heartbreaking fashion. Where had seven years gone by so fast?

Her shoes were new at least, yet another reason why to take extra blacksmithing duties on. Won't have no one say his daughter didn't have shoes to wear. She would be ready to go to the new school. He smoothed out the front of his black broadcloth suit, one of two he had befitting his new status as the mayor of a new town. His town. Milford, Georgia.

Carved out of the excesses of the large cotton plantation, Milford proper consisted of his smithy, a park in the town square planted with Mrs. Milford's favorite rose bushes, some resident cabins, and the train platform. Mrs. Milford was the only one who was left in the family in the main plantation house. The house, newly built after Sherman had come through, was not part of the town, but several miles due east. However, her imprint was there in the name and the rose bushes of the town.

Since Mrs. Milford believed in having Negroes lead their own, Virgil was her handpicked choice for mayor. His first act as mayor was to send for and greet the town's first schoolmaster, come to Georgia to teach the free and the formerly enslaved to read and write. Mrs. Milford made that all possible.

And he hated every single second of it.

The school master would be the one to find out that he was the very last person in this hamlet of six hundred or so God-fearing souls who should be the mayor. Even as he approached the platform, his heart pounded at being found out.

But when he and March rounded the corner to where the once-a-day train dropped off cargo and people and chugged on to Savannah, there was no schoolmaster waiting on the platform.

Instead, on the train bench, sat the most beautiful lady he had ever seen.

He would have been no less surprised if a colorful parrot or macaw from one of the Milford grandchildren's picture books came and lit on the wooden bench.

March took in a deep breath and he put his hand on her shoulder to steady her. His little daughter trembled at the sight of the lady.

His own stomach pitched around like ash at the edge of the fire. The lady leaned forward to regard them both. Her skin was the medium brown color of cooked oatmeal, the kind someone else made and not him, since he tended to scorch it.

And she flashed a smile to them with small, even teeth of the pearliest white.

Her cheeks had dimples that sunk in so charmingly he would have sworn his heart flipped upside down inside of his chest.

But almost as spectacular as she was in face, she was surrounded by yards and yards of black dress material, a dress so big and wide with hoopskirting, she tamed it down with small dainty hands as she stood to greet him.

Her black bonnet bobbed in kind as she greeted them with a pleasantly voiced "Good Day to you."

"She's so pretty." March breathed in.

She must be the schoolmaster's wife. Such a beautiful lady must be married to a high-up man like a schoolmaster. Where was the schoolmaster? No one emerged and instantly, he was made a fool in front of this beauty. He would have to speak to confirm it.

"Ma'am. We're here to meet the schoolmaster. Is he 'round this way?"

She regarded him with large eyes that resembled the candy chocolate drops Mrs. Milford kept in a big jar in the parlor. Her eyes were merry. "Are you Virgil Smithson?"

"I am."

He did not put out his hand as it would not be appropriate to shake hands with another man's wife. He had a daughter to raise and did not want to start trouble with the schoolmaster first off.

"I'm Amanda Stewart."

Virgil nodded. A nice proper name. "And your husband is getting your trunks?" Although it made no sense, a trunk should have been unloaded with them, but he saw nothing.

"I have no husband, sir. And I have no trunk."

"Your black dress?"

"For my father. Lawrence Stewart. I'm his daughter, Amanda. I've come to be the schoolteacher."

A rush of blood came into Virgil's ears and his heart threatened to beat right out of his chest.

"You? A schoolteacher?"

The lady, she said her name was Amanda? She rearranged her big skirt, big like how Mrs. Milford's used to be, and put her gaze on him. Something about her eyes, made her look as hopeful a little girl as March. "Yes, thank you Mr. Smithson. I've just finished the course at Oberlin College in Ohio. I've been my father's pupil for many years before that. Let me assure you, I'm well qualified."

"We wanted a man. Where is he?" Virgil blurted out and red heat blossomed onto his neck and face. She was sure to see it, no matter the deep brown of his skin tone. "Oh. So sorry for your loss."

The look on her delicate features etched deep pain. If she had been punched in the gut, she would have looked as hurt.

He wanted to collect her up and tell her it would be all right. "I'm sorry for your loss, miss." And he was sorry, but there was some terrible mistake.

"Thank you." She pulled a delicate white hanky out of a skirt pocket within the big skirt and wiped at her nose with it.

The whiteness of her hanky contrasted sharply with the deep jet of her gown and Virgil almost forgot his daughter in his discomfort until March said, "Pretty lady teacher."

And before he could stop it, Amanda Stewart bent down to talk with March, her big wide skirt spreading out into the dusty wooden platform. "Hello, I'm Miss Stewart."

"Pleased to meet you, Miss Stewart."

She bestowed that smile of hers on his little daughter and a connection knit itself between the lady and his child. No. Time to cut this off. He took March's hand in his. "The community sent for a male teacher, Miss."

Amanda stood and faced him again. This time he was surprised that the tip of her bonnet just about measured up to his chin. She carried herself much bigger than that. Or maybe it was her clothing. "You are mistaken, sir. The missive said you needed a teacher. I can provide that service."

He let go of March's hand and pointed down the road. "Most of them who needs the lessons is going to be old and big. Case you hadn't heard, freed slaves want to read and write. Got to stand up to them and not have no tinies talking to them just so."

He was a man who saved his eloquence in defense of God, especially when he prayed. He didn't know how to talk to some fancy Northern schoolteacher lady.

"Mr. Smithson. What are *tinies*?"

"Well, now…" Virgil spread his hands.

"Someone like me, ma'am. Small. Getting in the way. Daddy calls me a tiny sometimes. But I'm March. Mamma name me that so I know when I was born."

The lady inclined her head and looked down at March, her bonnet bobbing. "No tiny you, my child. You are a big girl. Even I can see that. A lovely spring child, just like your mamma named you."

"Got lots to do," Virgil interrupted. Wasn't too good for March to get big notions in her head. "And I don't have no time to watch over no schoolteacher lady."

"There have been women schoolteachers all over the South before and after the war, Mr. Smithson. I have my letter from the mission right here."

Virgil held up a hand. "I don't need to see no letter. And those women are widows. Or married. White ladies."

Silence lay between them.

March coughed.

The cast of her skin lit from within, shone incandescent. The recent loss in her life turned up in the deep wells that showed sharp cheekbones above the dimples. Did she have Indian blood? A mixed-blood lady teacher would have an even harder time. No, she had almost got him, but she had to go home. He picked up her case. "Well, I get you on to Pauline's and get you comfortable for the night. Bring you back here to meet the train in the morning."

If he had shot March with an arrow, he couldn't have wounded his daughter more, judging from the screwed-up look on her brown face. And made him all the more determined for this pretty lady to get on about her business. This woman with her fancy bonnet and her big trailing dress with the smallest possible waist put big ideas into March's head. What would he do with that once this lady was gone on about her rich life? Best to put all of that to an end. Now. Today. Well, at least tomorrow.

He moved off the platform, and March dragged her feet in her dusty shoes. But the rustle of the lady's skirts did not follow them.

Virgil turned. She was still up there on the platform, a dark bell against the afternoon sky.

"Got to walk. Town's up this way, Miss. Can't wait out here all night." If she stayed all night on the platform, he really would be responsible for her then. The thought of what could happen to her in the night made his dry throat catch.

"I'm staying right here, Mr. Smithson."

A stubborn female. An even worse sight for March to see.

He started again. "Nightfall come, Miss, and the night riders could come and do you great harm. Wouldn't want it to come to that."

Couldn't she see her safety was at stake? And he couldn't touch her to bring her on. He looked at March to see if she were concerned about this lady's safety, but his daughter, his own child, looked away from him.

Miss Amanda embodied danger itself. She had to go.

"I mean to say, I can't go anywhere else, Mr. Smithson. If you'll just take me to the teacher house, I'll be comfortable."

"I'm telling you, Pauline will put you up. What else you need to know?"

"I'm homeless, sir. I have no home or family or anywhere else to go."

He dropped her case to the dust, clean out of options and responses. No matter that he was a freeman who bought himself out of slavery way before the war come. A man who used fire to make iron bend to his will had just met his match.

CHAPTER TWO

"We going to find the right place for you to stay, ma'am," March told Amanda.

"Hush up, gal," March's father said as they moved on to Pauline's house. Whomever she was.

What was his name again? Virago… no, Virgil. Virgil Smithson. She could not reconcile the tall, fearsome bearded man in the pressed broadcloth suit with the name signed on the paper.

In person, he appeared like the picture of God on judgment day that used to be in the back of her primer. That book scared her silly for a good bit of her childhood, and it was probably a reason why she was not proficient to this day in that particular subject.

March squeezed her hand tighter, and the child's bones pressed into her hand with a sharpness. Had the child had a decent meal? Her heart plunged into her throat at the way the child had tried to dress herself up to meet her. March was not well-put together. Did her father have something to do with the awkward tilt of her braids and the shortness of her patched-together dress? Where was her mother?

Her thoughts could not linger long on those suppositions, because the hem of her black gown grew increasingly red with dirt as she walked. She hiked her skirts up a tad, but Virgil Smithson stared at her with a stern frown that made his mustache and small beard glint in the sunlight.

"Ladies wearing dresses like that don't walk in the dirt 'round here. They ride. Not a good use of dress."

"Well, sir, I wore what I have. I must wear mourning for my father."

He grunted. Grunted? Not very pleasant behavior, that. For a mayor. She tried to rearrange her face in a posture that did not judge, but she could not help herself. Father had been so refined a gentleman that she was not used to men who grunted, but she supposed they existed in this world.

He stopped walking, and they stood there in the middle of a roughly-hewn town square. The pink flowers along the edges certainly pleased the eye.

"What we doing, Papa?"

"Supposed to take the schoolmaster up to Mrs. Milford. She ain't him, so there's no need."

"I admit to a bit of train grime and some of this Georgia dust, but I assure you I will not embarrass anyone."

"She's a beautiful lady, Papa!" March fairly shouted.

"Thank you, honey." Amanda looked down into the sweet brown face of her new friend. It was good to have someone who cared, even if she was only six or seven years old.

"Won't take her on up to the Milfords looking like that."

"And how do you suggest I look, Mr. Smithson?"

He stared about him, paying her no attention. If the day weren't already so hot, she believed her blood would boil at his near-direct accusation.

Silence.

She repeated her question, lest he have a hearing impediment of some kind.

"Pauline must be in the fields. We got to get her to help."

"I don't know who Pauline is, but I don't want her help. If there is a basin of hot water, that will be sufficient."

Virgil Smithson put her case down and began to whistle and wave his arms. At his command, a bunch of young men came forward and surrounded him, jostling for position. What kind of Negro man was he who commanded that kind of respect? He towered above the rest of them, certainly.

The young men surrounded him, and he spoke to them in low, hushed tones so she could not hear. On purpose.

Very disrespectful. She pressed her lips together. A good deal of alarm on his part had to do with her arrival and staying, and this impromptu gathering with young Negro men dressed in a variety of dirty overalls, shirts, and work pants was most irregular. One by one, they disbursed from him, but as they did so, they gave her sidelong glances as if she were some kind of china doll. Which she wasn't. Virgil gave her a sidelong glance of contempt as he went away from them as well.

"I would like to freshen up please." She smoothed down her dress.

"Don't worry, Miss Lady," March informed her. "Papa just went to get Pauline to help you out of your present trouble."

She shook her head. "I'm not in any trouble. I just want to get to the house set aside for the teacher, so I can refresh myself. I have not come to be any trouble. I want to help." She squeezed the thin, small hand. "And my name is Miss Stewart."

"Miss Stewart. Hello." March tilted her head as she appraised her once more and threw her thin arms around a side portion of her skirt.

Amanda pulled the child's shoulders closer to her. Her heart did flips. She could feel March's shoulder blades through the white cotton dress she wore. "I believe it is time for some sustenance of some kind."

Virgil Smithson came and stood in front of them, arms folded. He pulled out a pocket watch and frowned. "Pauline be here soon."

If this man were the mayor, didn't he do anything himself? And who was this Pauline? His wife? Would he call his wife by her Christian name in front of her?

At the very thought of it, she breathed out a little, pressing on a stay stabbing her in the ribs and near determined to break through her corset. Virgil Smithson was a handsome man for women who liked that fierce, thundercloud kind of look. His eyebrows resembled raven's wings over his dark black eyes and surprisingly long, lush eyelashes. His cheekbones sunk in deep, and his beard and moustache were trimmed neatly. Everything thing about him, his derby hat, and his Prince Albert broadcloth suit proved him to be well-groomed and reflected on him as a personage in charge. An authority. His height helped too. His carriage resembled a tree—firm and direct. Probably just as reassuring to… to Pauline. Whoever she was. Amanda surely did not care.

They heard a small scuffling and flurry, and from around the corner, a little woman in a simple blue dress and spotless white kerchief came forth. She wore a beautiful bandana on her head and carried herself as a regal person would. Almost as regal as Virgil Smithson.

The woman went right up to Amanda and grabbed her hands. It was impossible to tell how old she was, but surely, in her height, she was only a few inches taller than March and came up to Amanda's elbow.

"You the schoolteacher?"

"I am. Are you Pauline?"

"Yes, child. Wonderful to have you here. Come on to my home and we'll freshen you up some. Can't have you looking just anyway, not when you so pretty, just come from the cold North and all."

Her insides warmed at Pauline's words. It was good to be welcomed and not treated as if she had a dread disease. "Thank you." And Pauline let her hands go to stand on the other side of her.

"She need to change out of that dress and put on something right." Virgil followed. "Then she can get on that train and go back where she come from."

"Virgil. This here is women's business. I don't see where you need to put your oar in the water to start rowing."

"Yes, ma'am." Amazed at the respectful tone in Virgil's voice, Amanda marveled. This woman seemed to be more of a mother figure. If Pauline was not his wife, who was?

"Get on back to work," Pauline directed him. "We'll see you at suppertime up to my house."

Scurrying off between a small child and a small woman, she stuffed her hands full of her dress to keep them stationary. *Thank you, God. I've been taken over so quickly in this strange place.* Still, she could not resist a look over her shoulder at the left-behind figure of Virgil Smithson who stood like a terrifying tree with his pocket watch in his hand, eyebrows drawn together as if judgment day was just around the corner.

There was a lot he had to learn about someone like her if they were to get along. Then again, she didn't come down south just to teach the children—she came to teach anyone who wanted to be taught.

Virgil could be first on the list.

Virgil had only returned to Milford last year, too long no doubt, but people here acted fool crazy over this so-called school-teacher with the big skirt.

Come stepping off of the train, thinking she's Mrs. Abe Lincoln or somebody high up. In all his born days, he never had seen anyone like this woman. She made his head hurt and a strange, quivery feeling start up in his stomach like he ain't had nothing to eat in days. Which wasn't true, because ever since he had come back, Pauline saw to it that he and March ate very well, which he paid her to do. Still, March was too thin and small for a child of her years. He meant to have her be fattened up.

Had Mrs. Milford cared for March while he was gone?

No time to think on that now. He ought to do as Pauline say and get back to the shop. If there weren't a couple of horses to be shod, he probably had mayor business to see about.

He would do it too, if it wasn't for this lady come in on the train playing fancy in her mourning dress. How could someone who looked like that have to come down here to find a place to be in the world?

Her skirt disappeared around the corner to where Pauline had taken her, and his apprentice, Isaac, came up to him. "That the teacher?"

He and Isaac moved with purpose back to the smithy. No time to be idle. Virgil pulled off his broadcloth coat and carefully hung it on the coat rack in the corner of the shop. It was a day to take off the shirtwaist to work, but he would just roll up the sleeves to the mid-portion of his arm. He didn't want to alarm anyone. His time away from Milford meant that he possessed a great deal of body strength, and he needed every bit of it to control the rages of his smithy.

The heat in the shop verged on unbearable, and he worked, drenched constantly in sweat, but at least the place was all his. It resembled the fiery pit of damnation, but he was proud of what he had accomplished. And he had accomplished it, despite great personal cost.

"Sent the wrong one. She need to get on the train back to where she come from and get on about her business up north." If he spoke it aloud, God would make it come to pass.

But she said she had no home. How could that be?

What had Miss Lady of the Bountiful Skirt accomplished? Anything in her spoiled, soft skinned, big saucer-eyed, soft-handed life? Probably nothing. A woman like that would melt down here in the hard South. And as mayor, this woman had become his problem. One that Mrs. Milford was not going to like or want to deal with.

"Line up these horses, boss?" Isaac said.

"Yeah. Ain't going to shod themselves."

"She was mighty pretty to watch, though. And got book learning. Why she have to go away?"

"Got to keep our minds on watching the fire and getting these horses taken care of. Can't be worried about no women just now."

"Need something pretty to look at 'round about these days."

Virgil fixed Isaac with a hard gaze, but his apprentice did not seem to mind. "Pretty is as pretty does. Nothing worse than a vain woman. And you got Pauline to look at. Mind that."

"I know. But she teaches folk to read. And, well, I never thought about learning to read. But if she's teaching the children, maybe..." Isaac's voice wandered off, still not paying proper attention.

"Maybe what?"

He didn't want the young man to cower. Virgil knew he had a stern way about him; it was one of the things Sally was always telling him about himself. But just now, Isaac was about too much good timing and not enough working. And here he had already wasted half the day, picking up this teacher who wasn't even what the community needed.

"Nothing, boss man."

"See to it. Bring in that filly. Horse needs proper shoes to make sure she working right. No extra time to be wondering about getting reading lessons. Do that on your own time."

"Yes, sir. Just thought, now we can do what we want, maybe we want to read."

"Read what? You learning a fine trade here. Been a free man blacksmithing all my life. Saved up enough money to buy my Sally up out of it. Ain't nowhere you can go where folks don't need a smithy."

"Smithing is a fine profession," Isaac echoed.

"Be sure you know it too."

"Man can't work all the time, though, sir." Isaac said it in the most pleasant voice he had. The lack of a smile on his face proved he meant what he said. "Man should make a nice living and then find a nice wife and get settled down somewhere. I wants to work for myself."

"Well, first you work for me," he told his apprentice, meaning to sound jovial. Didn't work. Laughing and joking never came natural to him.

"Beg pardon, sir."

Isaac brought forward a dappled gray, petting her down her forelock, and handed the horse off. Virgil touched the horse's withers, reaching for a carrot to help calm her. He grasped her leg and put it in the target spot between his knees. A large part of smithing was getting the horses calm so their shoes could be changed without too much difficulty.

"God and a woman. That's who ought to boss a man," Isaac said with certainty.

Virgil nodded, determined to work.

"Milfords was okay to us and all, but we wasn't free."

"Wasn't around here enough to know." Virgil patted the horse down again. "Calm down, lady."

"Good thing. Sally slaved for that woman a long, long time."

Isaac's words stopped him. Anything stopped him when the talk was about March's mother.

"I know." He pulled the calm horse's hoof to him, and the gray let him hew the hardened nail away to pry off the old shoe. "I know."

"Sally died not knowing what you done for her."

"She think..." He patted the horse to calm it. Well, and himself too. "She think I left her all by herself for good. That I was no good."

"Everyone know you be back."

"Georgia didn't let no free people stay. Couldn't stay with my wife and child, no matter how much I wanted." He wanted to pound a shoe so bad just now. But he was at the point of getting the horse's old shoe off. Without hurting this skittish lady.

"She knew. And that's how come Mrs. Milford ain't said nothing."

So Mrs. Milford's silence had met its goal—to divide him from Sally for the rest of his life. And if Mrs. Milford knew about this new lady schoolteacher, she would find a way to put a stop to that as well.

Which might actually work well for him. They'd be together on something for once. Pretty pampered thing like Amanda

Stewart, she see how hard life was down here and she would forget all about teaching a school and go running back up to where she come from. He'd make sure of it.

He pried up the shoe from the horse's foot with an implement and pared away the hoof to get an even level. "Beat the shoe out."

He tossed the horse's shoe back to Isaac who caught it with the long pliers and laid it in the heat. His loud taps against the anvil rang out and echoed in the small old barn. Isaac stopped when the shoe was evened out and plunged it in the water to cool. Steam rose up from the water pit, and a twinge of discomfort plucked at him. Silence was a comfort usually, but the annoying thought about Amanda Stewart's presence stirred him inside.

"I don't want that teacher coming up in here ruining my daughter. Putting ideas into her head."

"How she going to ruin her? She can teach her things about being a fine colored woman, maybe teach her to be a schoolteacher."

Isaac retrieved the shoe and held it before him for inspection. Virgil shook his head, and Isaac laid it in the fire again, hammering hard to thin it out some more. He held it up again before plunging it into the water pit, and this time Virgil approved and took up the cooled shoe.

He had to put it to Isaac so he would understand. So that anyone would understand. "No. March stay here with her family." Blood family was too rare to loose.

"You know Sally didn't want March doing all her life for Mrs. Milford. She want her to learn to read and write. You promised her before you leave."

"Isaac. What you remember? You was just a tiny then."

"I'm March's uncle. Sally's baby brother. And I got to see that you do right by her child."

"I know." A tug of irritation pulled at him. Was it because Isaac sought to remind him that he was actually family to Sally and March and not just claim kin? Or was it because Isaac didn't do the shoe right the first time?

"God brung that teacher down here to help us. To help March. She'll bring something special to the place. You'll see."

If Mrs. Milford didn't first see that the younger woman was better dressed than her. And if she did… well, that would solve Virgil's problem, wouldn't it?

Somehow, the prospect didn't make him feel much better. The thought of the schoolteacher getting on the train to go out into nothingness, without a home or friend in the world, made his fingers stiff, not wanting to bend to work.

Retrieving the first shoe from the pit, and readying the nails to attach it, Virgil neglected to pat down the gray and she balked. Got to focus when working on a horse—they could sense turmoil going on in a man's mind, sure enough. 'Specially a female horse. He patted her forelock, and she calmed down.

Isaac had done a good job this time. Using five nails, he attached the shoe and when he let her leg down, he imagined the horse was grateful. He patted her to show he understood.

There had to be a way of helping Miss Stewart and being shed of her.

The horse's feet danced all around his, eager for relief to get her other shoes changed. He made sure to stay out of the way. Didn't need to be laid up with a broken toe or foot. Lots to do here, and a rumble of irritation stirred through his fingers. He was behind because of the time he took to meet the lady schoolteacher. A lady they didn't even need.

The gray kept on dancing and he patted her down. Better to focus on the grateful gray filly and the work ahead. He couldn't afford any more women coming into his life seeking to destroy him, including this here filly, impatient with her dancing sore feet.

He would figure it all out by supper time.

CHAPTER THREE

When Amanda got to Pauline's house, the problem was evident. Her skirts were too wide.

She wanted to sink through the rich red clay. Would she be able to get through the door? How foolish she must appear to these people with her entirely impractical clothes.

March stood next to her, bouncing on her toes, eager to have her come inside.

She looked around the neat front yard and whispered to the little woman. "Is there somewhere I could put something on? Out here?"

Pauline stopped short and witnessed, to her shame, Amanda's predicament. "Go on over into the barn, see there? And take off your crinoline. That will help out."

March guided her to the barn. Fortunately, there were no animals there to witness her complete shame and disgrace. But March was.

"Dear March, do you have somewhere you have to be?"

"No. Daddy lets me run all day long. That's why we're so glad you're here, so I can be in school learning and not being a tiny underfoot to poor Pauline."

Maybe talking to the child would keep her occupied. Amanda hiked up the lengths of black bombazine into her hands to access the tapes on the crinoline cage. "What do you think you would like to learn?"

"Papa says I should learn lady things like sewing, cooking, churning, and such."

"Do you know how to read yet?" Four more tapes to go.

"No, but I've always wanted to hear a story. Papa tells stories about the Bible when we have meetings and they're pretty interesting."

"Well, there will be a lot of that going on." Two more to go, including the one at the top. March seemed most fascinated by what she was doing. "Storytelling is a part of school."

"And got to do figuring. That's a big important thing to learn."

It was. And she would just have to endure the humiliation of the child. Swiftly with shaking fingers, she undid the last tape about her waist and shook the material down her front and stepped out of the cage. The cage stood next to her, looking strange and incongruous in the barn, but she'd attained liberty. *Praise God.* She pressed again on the little bone in her corset which poked her, and turned to the door, only to see March appear to be a bit diminished.

"What is it, child?"

"Well, miss. It just seems like the dress is all sad now without that under it." March pointed to the cage. "It was happy before, dancing and swinging, and now you not. Just look like everyone else 'round here."

"Such a beautiful word picture you've told me, March. Almost like a poem." She stared down at her waist and her heart turned over at the yards and yards of black fabric in her hands. Such a waste of material.

She grabbed handfuls of it out of the dust and faced March's bedraggled little countenance again. "I never really looked at my dresses before. They are certainly big, aren't they?"

"Yes, miss. Like a smile."

Beautiful. Well, it was good to count one friend among her acquaintance here, no matter how short of a time she would stay—according to the child's father. Amanda untied the ribbon holding the bonnet on her head and took it off as well. She would just hold her bonnet in her hand since she had no hat box anymore. She'd sold off most of what she'd possessed but had kept this little plain bonnet and decorated it just a bit. It wouldn't have been right to have it be any more than what it was, knowing her father's penchant for modesty.

The old pain sliced through her again, remembering her father was buried on a hill in Ohio and she was so far away from him in Georgia.

March inhaled again and looked timid. "May I hold your hat, miss?"

"Of course you may, March." She leaned down and handed it to the child, who touched the bonnet with trembling fingers.

"You got braids like me."

"My braids are arranged in a bun." She patted her bun and the gathered braided hair whorls on the side of her head. Braiding it up was a good way to keep it in control during the day. Other women of her acquaintance wanted to flatiron their hair, but she knew what a disaster that could be. A woman could be burned. It was better to flat braid it.

"Think mine will do that someday?" March asked.

She put the bonnet on the little girl's head. "I have no doubt, March. You already look like me. Let's go see what Miss Pauline says for us to do."

When they went out of the barn, they greeted Pauline in the swept-up yard who was on her way out. "I've got to get back to the fields. Every minute count just now. I put some dinner on the table for you both." She pointed at March. "And you watch supper on the back of the stove."

"Thank you for your help."

"I'm glad you here so our children can get to learn." Pauline patted her arm and scurried off behind the house.

"My, she's very busy." Amanda moved forward. "Let's see what's for dinner."

Two tin mugs of buttermilk sat on the table, accompanied by two bowls, each with a hunk of cornbread down in it. She clutched at the extra fabric of her dragging dress to refrain from commenting.

"My favorite!" March sat down and pulled a bowl closer.

Her favorite? Where was the meat? The vegetables? Didn't March expect any? Amanda's eyes smarted as she reflected on her father's discussions at dinners they had shared. Having been an ardent abolitionist, he'd made sure that his only child grew up understanding the horrors of slavery. To stay safe and to avoid kidnapping into the institution were the mainstays of his prayers, and he prayed for those things nightly.

But she never expected to come up close to the actual institution. And this was March's favorite dinner. "Have you washed your hands and face, young lady?"

March slid down off of the hewn pine chair and went outside to a pump. Amanda looked around at the sink in the one room cabin and saw only a carved wooden basin propped up in the corner. No water pump there. She went out to where March sluiced her hands in the cold water. Putting her own hands in the stream of cold water, she splashed her face. March did the same, then shook the water pellets off and smiled at her. Dear child. They quickly saw to their rough ablutions and went back inside.

"Dear God," she intoned after they sat down to the plain meal, "we ask you for your blessings upon this food, this house, and this child. We have started on a new path in your glory, God. Please let me be the party of your choosing to reflect that glory, whether it be here or elsewhere."

And despite the lingering heat inside the small cabin, she trembled. Surely it could not have been in God's plan for her to become a soiled dove in the clutches of Charles Henry. *Please, God, help me stay here.*

"Keep my new schoolteacher here with me. Amen, dear God."

"Thank you, March." She opened her eyes and faced the child who blinked at her with her sweet button eyes. But her face was too thin. "Eat up, child. We need to find a way to be productive today. God would have us help Him in His work in the world."

March ate so eagerly and completely of her mashed up corn-bread and buttermilk that Amanda slipped her half of her portion and still had a hard time finishing what was before her. The mean fare was fine, but it was hard to get food past the perpetual lump in her throat. What was going to happen to her? Her life was in the hands of Virgil Smithson, and she had to convince him, somehow, that she could help the newly formed community to thrive. She used the spoon to scrape the last bit of cornbread from the bowl and forced it down with a sip of the lukewarm buttermilk. She refused to combine them in the bowl as March did.

"Now. Should we tidy up your house? See the schoolhouse? Make a new dress for you?"

"My house? That's on the other side of the fields, ma'am, and Papa wants me to stay close to him while he's smithing. That's rule number one."

"It's good to hear that you listen to your father. Honor thy mother and father." She repeated the commandment, and it felt good on her lips. The honor was to her father, and she was here. *I must make good on it.*

"Schoolhouse is over by us. Papa works on it whenever he can. It's just about done. Made a schoolhouse and a house for the teacher together. So I can't go over there now, cause of what Papa say."

"I understand. We'll stay here until we've got something different to do."

"You say you make me a dress?"

"We can start on that. I have my sewing bag with me. We can make something pretty for you."

"Ain't got no cloth. Got to go to Crumpton for that."

They had cloth. She was wearing it. Looking at how Pauline was dressed and how March was dressed, the way she looked wasn't going to work out very well in Milford. And given the yards and yards of fabric in her own dress, she could sacrifice some of it to make a dress for March and reform smaller hoops from her crinoline cage. Or go without as Pauline did.

Maybe looking as if she fit in might help Virgil Smithson see she belonged.

Not that she cared what he thought, just as long as it helped her stay.

"Fetch my bag, child. Everything we need is in there. Let's clear off the table so we can make a pattern."

"I never had a dress made for me before." March jumped up to clear away the dishes and take them out to the pump. Faster than she thought, March brought them back in and then lugged in Amanda's valise, which had her sewing bag in it. She wasn't sure she had put it in there. *Thank you, God.*

"Where did you get the pretty one you're wearing now?" She stood in front of March, looking at the bedraggled thing that was once white.

"Mrs. Milford got granddaughters. They grow out of their stuff, and bring it for me when they come to visit. They my friends."

"I'm sure. Let's take this off and put on a special little dress we call a slip in the meantime. We have to stay inside while we do this, but when you make a dress, you need a pattern. We'll cut the pieces a little bigger than what they are, because you are growing into a big, big girl and won't be a tiny much longer."

She tied one of her petticoats around March's slight body, and folded up the hem so that she didn't trip. Then she stepped out of the black bombazine. With a sigh, she took her small sewing scissors and detached the bodice and the skirt. Once she did that, and ripped up a seam on the skirt, it was clear that she had been wearing entire lengths of fabric on her person.

"Here we go, March." With determined snips, she cut the skirt of the dress in half. The actions made her feel lighter already.

They worked together very well all afternoon. March's dear little chatter kept her occupied and from feeling the horrible sharp ache of missing her father. The ache would hit her right in her midsection and take the breath from her body.

Breathe. She must keep breathing, for him. Still, if her father had known about the nefarious purpose of Charles Henry—

"What's happening here?"

She shifted in her chair at the thunder-deep voice at the door. Virgil Smithson. And she was in her slip.

Well, maybe more than that. She wore the bodice of her dress, and Virgil could only see her from the waist up. Still, on her lower half, she wore her petticoats. No man had ever seen her in her petticoats. The purpose of this entire enterprise was to prevent a man from seeing her in her petticoats.

March ran to her father. "We making me a dress."

"You got a dress."

"Miss Stewart, she making me another dress. Out of her dress. So it won't be so big." March waved her arms in excitement, but her father paid her no attention.

"You need to go put on your dress. Now."

"It's not put together yet," Amanda put in.

"What you done with her dress?"

She gulped. But she straightened up and stared Virgil Smithson in the eye, in spite of the fact that her lower half was only clothed in a petticoat. "I took it apart to use as a pattern. If you wait for a few minutes—"

The soul-deep voice cut her off. "I want my child in the dress she came in. Now."

"Excuse me, Mr. Smithson, but I'm not a child and I won't be spoken to as if I am one."

They faced off, him in the doorway, she sitting at the table and so desperately wanting to stand to press her point. But she couldn't.

Since she only wore petticoats.

She probably couldn't stand anyway, since her knees shook at the thought of this man, or any other for that matter, seeing her in her petticoat.

This enterprise to obtain a living for herself was off to a beautiful and wonderful start.

Why was his child parading around in underclothes? This was what happened when she spent an afternoon with this Miss Stewart? What kind of teacher would this woman be? Seemed hard to make heads or tails of why March was wearing a fine lacy petticoat tied up around her stick-skinny self and why this fancy lady sewed on black cloth squares.

The ways of females were a complete mystery to him, and he hoped they remained so. The dress Mrs. Milford gave them torn up and apart. How was that better for his daughter?

Now this stranger spoke to him in a way many people did not. After all, he was the mayor. "Didn't say you were a child. I just said I want my daughter in her own clothes is all."

"And we will sew them back together as quickly as we can. Please sit over by the fire."

Miss Stewart gestured from her chair as if she was the Queen of England. And in Pauline's cabin too. Wait 'til she came in from the fields to see all this happening.

"March," came the evenhanded high tone of Miss Stewart's voice, "gather the portions of your old dress together, and I'll baste them together so you may leave for home."

"We ain't in no hurry. We usually eats supper here first and then goes home. That why I been stirring them beans on the back of the stove. That's supper with some more cornbread."

"I see. Your father gives the impression you had to go back to your own home for your own supper." A smooth eyebrow rose and regarded him as he sat in the rocking chair by the fire.

"Papa and I don't cook. Ain't no food there. Pauline give us food and Papa pay her to feed us or take care of her farm here."

"This lady don't need to know all of our affairs," he barked. Silence fell in the room.

Amanda raised an eyebrow at him. "Bring the pieces here, child."

"Do as she say, so you can wear your own things."

The frown on March's face pressed deep into her small face. He expected to be obeyed when he said something and didn't want to hear female chatter about it. This woman was already a bad influence and had March clothed in a whole lot of fancy petticoats. They didn't have so much extra for ruffly, frilly petticoats, and March should not get used to such foolishness.

The fire crackled as Amanda Stewart bent to her task, sewing with a line across her lips, as if the very devil were on her tail. A disappointment, since the luscious fullness of her lips disappeared.

He broke the silence that had landed on them all. "I'll get some more firewood." Seems as if March was having a good time before he came and ruined it. He didn't mean to. He had done enough to destroy March's good times.

He went out to the woodpile. Pauline came from the fields, holding her hoe.

Pauline had been Sally's best friend and comfort. It was Pauline who had taken in March when Sally got sold away, Pauline who had washed and dressed Sally's body for burial. Now she took care of them both. What would he be without her? Lost. It was one reason why he took on her young husband as an apprentice—so Pauline might not have to work so hard someday.

"What you doing out at the woodpile?" Pauline's eyes sparkled. "You been misbehaving?"

If it hadn't been for the high flying teacher in there, he might have been embarrassed. "They in there sewing. She went to make March a dress and went and took apart the dress Mrs. Milford gave her."

Pauline inhaled a breath. "She sewing it back together."

"Yeah. Got my child dressed in a fine petticoat while she working."

"She could be wearing worse. Dress was old. If she can sew, that's good. Lots of folks need mending and such around here. I know I don't have time to do it, since I got to work this land."

It hadn't occurred to him that Miss Stewart could be performing a useful task. "It's no good to have my child in a fancy petticoat."

"You don't like that teacher, do you?" Pauline stood there, nodding her head, seeming like she was having fun.

"That's not what I asked for."

"God don't always give us what we ask for. God give us what we need. You the preacher 'round here, you should know. And March needed a new dress. We need a teacher. We got one. I don't see the difference."

Pauline always made plain sense.

"She a woman."

"Who can sew. I need to step in here and see what she can make me out of my petticoat. 'Cept I ain't got one." Pauline winked at him and went around to the front of her house to go inside.

He winced. Why she go and tell him that? Was that the price to be paid for having a daughter—to learn about all of these female things he didn't know about?

The rumble in his stomach rose up louder at the smell of the beans on the back of Pauline's stove. That was a better supper than what he might have prepared. How long would it take to put together March's dress? He stood and kicked at the dirt, then picked up the wood, ready to put some inside the woodbox.

A small boy came running up and stopped in front of him, bent over double, grasping at his knees. He breathed heavily as he spoke. "Miz. Milford. She say—"

"Calm down, Caleb. What she say?"

"Missy. Mrs. Milford. She say she want to meet the strange lady what come on the train."

How did Mrs. Milford find out about this woman? This town was like a bucket with a hole in the bottom. Couldn't hold nothing.

"She say to bring her up to the house."

"When?"

"Tomorrow morning. 'Bout nine."

Train was due at ten. Why did Mrs. Milford want to see her anyway? He would take Miss Stewart up there in his wagon and bring her down to the platform to catch that ten o'clock train. Probably leave her valise at the platform so she could make it on time, since the train wouldn't come back through again until Monday morning.

No matter what, Miss Amanda Stewart needed to be on the train and out of Milford at ten in the morning. He would see to it.

CHAPTER FOUR

Did this woman even know how to behave in front of someone like Millicent Milford?

Virgil's hands went slick with sweat as he bore witness to the patched mess of March's dress. *Lord, what have you visited upon us?* He guessed that she could tell by his confused look that he wasn't pleased.

"You told me to patch her together and I did." Amanda folded her arms and made a face. Her nose turned up just a little at the end, an interesting feature he had never seen before on any Negro woman. Must be the Indian blood. Which tribe?

"You the one sewing. Put the dress together right."

"And you, Mr. Smithson, should say what you mean. Come here, child." Amanda coaxed the patched-together dress off of March.

Meanwhile, Pauline made little laughing snorts in the corner. What did she find so funny? She stopped her snorting and spoke out to them. "You all might as well eat supper here. You stay too so you can be proper ready for your visit up to Miss Milly in the morning."

He drew his eyebrows together. Ever since he came back, he made a pledge to have a home for his daughter and to have her be sheltered and protected under her own roof. It was one thing to take meals somewhere in the small town, something else completely different to have to stay there because March's one good dress was tore up. All because of what Miss Northern Woman thought she would do.

"Don't see what was wrong with the other dress anyhow."

"It was getting too small. I growing right out of it, Miss Amanda say. A wild-growing spring child."

"Yes, March." Amanda bent to her task with a mindful focus. She took a few swift stitches in the cloth and looked up at him. "Also, it's not her dress."

"What you mean it's not her dress?"

"It belonged to someone else first."

He nearly had to cover his mouth to prevent an owly hoot from coming out. "Let me let you know. Just a bit back, us people wouldn't have minded wearing a cast-off dress, too small or not."

"That's not how it has to be now."

He opened his mouth and shut it again. Did this woman even understand reason?

"Miss Milly see that dress look all tore up like that, she wouldn't like it."

"She gave the dress away. What does she care what happens to it after that? Especially if her granddaughter can get no use of it anymore. Why does it matter?"

Miss Lady had a point. It shouldn't really matter. But it did. Her coming down here, mixing things up didn't make it right.

"Every young lady should have something of her own."

A small smile of encouragement passed between his daughter and the stranger. He grimaced as he bore witness to the swift friendship they had after only a couple hours in each other's company. But wasn't Pauline enough of a female companion?

And March's aunt, to boot? He had thought her enough female company, but maybe he was wrong.

He could taste the relief he felt when Pauline called them to the hearty fare of beans and bacon. *Fill my stomach with your bounty, Lord*, he prayed. *Got to steel myself with what's to come.* This strange woman had him all turned around, inside out and upside down.

After he blessed the food, he made a silent plea of his own. *God, prepare me for your will.*

These women kept telling him, in pure female foolishness, that because she tore March's dress and her own, they would have to be there into the night. Thankfully Pauline was a good sport about putting some pallets down for him and March to sleep on. Isaac would sleep in the barn. Miss Lady got to sleep on the spare tick bed Pauline had, to be able to stay up and finish her dress business.

Morning dawned bright and clear, but when Virgil woke up, he felt as crooked and as wrong, like a child's jigsaw.

Sleeping on hard wood floors was nothing new to him. But he hadn't done it in more than a year, and getting up off the floor, the cricks in his neck and back stabbed at him like knives. Pauline, especially, smiled to see his painful torment.

Didn't mean the same thing to little March, though, since she got up all sprightly as usual and did her usual dancing around in the morning, looking like the spit of Sally.

"Praise God," he greeted her.

"Praise God, Papa," March shouted.

He put a finger to his lips to silence her and led the way out of the cabin, past Pauline and Amanda who were still sleeping.

A laugh bubbled up inside of him. He hurried outside so he wouldn't laugh indoors. Miss Lady with the mixed-up blood and turned-up nose actually snored. Quiet ones, but snores nonetheless.

He and March washed up in the cold pump water. When they went back in the cabin, both Pauline and Miss Lady were dressed.

Virgil eyed her. Yes, now she would do.

The silhouette was much smaller, but more refined and stately. She'd looked like a show bird before, but now she was appropriately toned down. She held up the dress for March next to her, and his daughter ran eagerly over to grab at the dress. "Manners."

"Thank you, Miss Stewart."

March's lit-up face and eyes at her own dress nearly knocked him to his knees. He cleared his throat and spoke.

"Thought it would take more time."

"I stayed up to get it done."

"It's black."

"Yes. I got the fabric from my dress." She spoke in soft measured tones, like he couldn't understand. Embarrassment at her words reached inside and squeezed at his pride.

"Thank you for explaining, Miss."

"Amanda. My name is Amanda."

"Don't address people I don't know by their first names. Especially not young women. I got manners."

"Clearly, Mr. Smithson. It just seemed to me that you had an aversion to my name."

He didn't know what she was talking about, but he would ignore that. "Miss will do. You aren't going to be here long anyhow."

He ignored the pained look on her face. He also had to overlook how he gripped at his fingers as he said them. Anyone who had dresses like that would be okay in the world. Wasn't his problem.

"I'm twenty-one. I am capable of keeping track of my where-abouts. Thank you, Mr. Smithson."

Pauline and March stood there, staring at them while they sniped at each other's heels like a pack of dogs. Pauline coughed and spoke. "I made some breakfast for you all if you hungry."

A wave of shame washed over him, but as March's father, he had the last words. "Children don't belong to wear black. Make them look like they're ready for the grave."

He sat down to the table, pulled up his plate of sweet mush, and poured water from the pitcher into a mug. Long day ahead. He needed to be ready to help Miss Lady on down the road of her life.

"Is that all you have to say?" Amanda demanded. The sharp cricks in her neck from staying up and sewing much of the night tormented her, and her capacity to be polite dwindled by the minute.

Virgil sat at the table, shoveling in still-warm mush as if his life depended on getting that food into his belly.

Pauline tapped her on her shoulder. "Virgil don't say much. Save all his words for preaching the Lord's word. On Sunday."

"He preaches?"

"Oh, yes. No one preach up like Virgil."

"So you're a preacher as well?"

He spoke around a mouthful of mush. "That's what she say."

"Compelling." She slid into her chair and helped March sit at the table.

"I don't know what you're talking about, but we serve God here in Milford."

"Yes, I appreciate that." She took small dainty bites of the mush, which was not sweet enough. It was enough to be able to swallow it.

"You familiar with God's Word?" She didn't take gravy with her mush either. Why not?

"Very." She could be a woman of few words as well. When she needed to be.

"Hmm. We need to see what you know."

"Hard to do, Mr. Smithson, when I am to leave in a few hours."

"You right about that."

"Best wait to see what Miss Milly has to say," Pauline said.

"Why is that?" Amanda regarded Pauline, puzzling.

"Virgil the mayor of our small town. But this is still the land that the plantation was once. She got a lot of say. Best wait to hear from her." She patted March's cheek. "I put the beans on again. You watch them." She turned to Amanda. "You. Take care of yourself. Know that the Lord orders your steps."

Amanda nodded. She tried to keep that uppermost in her mind, but it was nice to have a reminder of it. "Thank you."

Completely unexpected, Pauline patted her cheek.

"Thank you." Her eyes stung with unshed tears. God would provide her with protection, enough protection that she did not end up in the clutches of Charles Henry again.

Virgil spoke up, clearly uncomfortable at these shows of affection toward her. "Need to finish breakfast so we can get going."

Pauline waved as she walked out the door, and the reassuring female presence that had been protection from this grunting preacher man disappeared.

Amanda sought to fill the empty void with mush, but the gesture didn't work very well.

Did Miss Lady see through him? Virgil wouldn't put it past her. She did have special high-up education. Who understood what went on in one of those Northern colleges? He had traveled far and wide, but he'd never chanced to find out.

Time she got on with her life. Probably go out and find a teacher man or something, somebody to take care of her. He'd buy her lots of big skirts and be his pretty wife with lots of bouncing bonnets to surround her dimpled sandy-colored cheeks and turned-up nose.

"Best get on." He straightened himself from the table. "March, clean on up."

"Take care not to disturb your pretty frock. I'll tie an apron on you." Amanda jumped up and pinned a white towel on top of March's new black dress.

These women were about more foolishness than he could understand. "She not coming with us. She'll be right here."

"Oh? Why not?"

"I'm her father. I say she staying here to clean up."

"March is not a servant. I'm sure she would be up for the trip."

"Miss, you need to learn how to stay out of things that you know nothing about. March don't need to go up to see Miss Milford. She want to see you. That's what the boy said."

He turned on a heel and walked out the door. There was a great deal to see in this big country called America, but you sure didn't have to go far to find a fool. Not that Amanda Stewart was one, but how did she grow up? How did she grow up and not know about not showing yourself in front of a white person unless you got called for?

Time was, getting called to see someone like Mrs. Milford wasn't no game. Might be in trouble. Might be called in to hold you back while somebody you love got sold off. Could be any number of *might bes.* No, it was always best to stay in the background, stay out of sight, and don't remind rich, powerful folk like the Milfords of what they had. And he wasn't seeking to remind her about March.

Sally had been Mrs. Milford's favorite handmaid, everyone thought. Before she got sold off. March looked a great deal like her mamma, and the less Mrs. Milford was reminded about Sally and what he tried to do, the better. He just got to be mayor here, and it was best not to stir the pot. Bad enough that this Amanda Stewart come along. The sooner Miss Lady was gone out of their community, the better. Guess she did do something nice, getting March a new dress and all. March did seem to like her. And she said she didn't have no place to go.

But someone who didn't even know how to act in front of a plantation mistress? No. She was nothing but trouble, all day long.

The sad look on March's face overwhelmed her, but at least the child had on something that fit her. A small accomplishment in the short time she was there. "Bloom where you're planted," her father reminded her.

Virgil Smithson would see to her transplantation.

Still, her heart warmed because March's long legs looked less stick thin in a dress that fit.

"Be a good girl, March, and honor thy father."

"Yes, Miss Stewart. It was nice knowing you the short time you was here in Milford. I be okay. I got a dress of my own to wear." She reached up and patted Amanda's cheek in the same way Pauline had done.

Virgil pulled a wagon in front of the house. Amanda eyed the seat. Even though her dress was smaller now, the front seat was still high up.

He held out a hand for her.

She would have to take it. But she had no gloves on. She had sold them, thinking them an unnecessary luxury. Now she had to face the prospect of touching Virgil Smithson.

And he stared at her, the frown firming across his thick brows, clearly unhappy at the prospect of touching her.

Maidens were not supposed to touch men outside her family with any familiarity, but she had to get in that wagon to plead her case to Mrs. Milford.

Taking in a breath and biting the inside of her lip, she laid her hand in his lightly. He grabbed her hand, and a jolt of warmth shot through her, nearly knocking her in her middle.

She thought the pain of losing her father was intense. This, this feeling was far more intense and discomforting.

"Excuse me," Virgil said. Had he felt it too?

Well, at least he had the good grace to say that. But he did not let her hand go, and she understood that she must press up to get into the wagon. So she did, through all of that feeling, and managed to keep her smaller hoops neatly in place. *Thank you, God. But please warn me the next time.*

The next time she what? Touched him?

Instead of looking at him, she kept her eyes on March's long, lean, and disappointed face as she waved to them, riding away on the wagon box.

Now there must be silence between them, for who could explain what had just happened? Only the Almighty himself knew, and he certainly wasn't letting on.

"Fine day," Virgil said.

Oh, now he could be bothered to talk with her, since he was on the verge of being rid of her. She wouldn't give him the satisfaction. No. She folded her arms and looked straight ahead. She would not speak.

But he was correct. The rolling green of the Georgia countryside reflected lovely sunshine while large trees bearing white flowers surrounded the road. They turned onto a wider path, and a large home loomed before them, an inlet of water shining blue in the sun. The water looked like fine jewelry, indeed.

She could not help herself. To be silent was to ignore God's blessing. "Oh, this is so beautiful."

"Nothing like Milford up there in the north?"

"No. No. This is truly a reflection of God's glory."

He looked at her with surprise." Always thought so. Tried to stay away. Had to at one point. But no one leaves Milford for long."

"Ha. Well then, I guess I will be staying." She hoped it were true.

He only grunted. Before she left, she would let him know that grunting was not a way human beings communicated with one another.

Virgil pulled up in front of the large home. "Nobody's here?"

"Who should be here?"

"Charles, the butler at least."

She shivered at the name. It was all too common.

Virgil jumped off of the wagon box with an easy grace and came around to her side. He held out both hands. "I got you."

"I'm afraid not, Mr. Smithson."

"Ain't no way for you to climb out of that wagon box but to jump. Come on now."

"I will not. There must be a stool or something."

"There ain't. Come on. Ain't got all day and the train come in an hour."

He just couldn't wait to remind her of that, could he? Amanda turned to him and tried to take control of her body so it wouldn't collide with his, but instead, his big hands closed in around her waist, spanned it, and lifted her out as if she were a treasure.

The jolt between them came again but ebbed in intensity as he set her on the ground. When he removed his hands from her person, she brushed at the prickles dancing in her skin. "Thank you, Mr. Smithson."

"Welcome."

She adjusted her bonnet so she couldn't see him regard her. "This way?"

"We don't go in the front door."

"I don't see why not." She stepped forward, but he held her back.

"We go 'round back."

"Well, you didn't pull up there. You pulled up in front."

Virgil exhaled a breath as he let her go, and the intense feeling where he'd touched her went away. "You trying to get us killed here."

"Will anyone see us?"

"Mrs. Milford. She'll know."

"And will she kill us?"

She tilted her head sideways to see his face. The thunder-god reigned there. But at the corner of his well-formed lips, a small hint of a smile lingered. His lips had a nice shape and color, just edged with a slight tempting slice of pink. Like a strawberry.

What am I thinking? She retreated back into safety, back into her bonnet.

The problem of where to enter resolved itself when a petite figure crowned with neatly braided white hair appeared at the large front door and came out onto the large wide porch. "Virgil. Here I am. I thought we could meet out here on the veranda. It's a fine day, isn't it? And I know you have work to do in the town."

"Yes, I do. Good to see you today, ma'am." Virgil's voice resonated deep and respectful, but with self-assurance. Still, the slight, small carriage of Mrs. Milford was so welcoming that Amanda startled to think of this woman running such a large plantation home.

"Been some time, hasn't it?" Millicent Milford walked to a corner of the veranda where chairs had been placed around a small wooden table with a tray of cookies on it. "Come. Sit in the shade."

Amanda walked beside Virgil and stood just at the edge of his shadow. Mrs. Milford's gaze swept up and down her person "Well, who is this?"

"This here is Miss Amanda Stewart. She say the mission society send her to teach the school in the town."

"Well. A lady teacher. A pretty thing too, isn't she?"

"Suppose so, ma'am." Virgil regarded her with a sidelong glance, showing his contempt for her, she supposed.

That was a nice thing for him to say, wasn't it?

"Welcome to Milford Farm, dear. Have a seat."

"Thank you, Mrs. Milford."

"Lovely manners as well. I notice you are in mourning. Had you lost a sweetheart in the last days of the war?"

"No, ma'am. My father. Just a few weeks ago."

"So sorry to hear, child. You're so pretty, I thought it might have been a sweetheart. My condolences. It's hard to lose a parent."

"Her daddy was the expected schoolteacher. That's who we wanted." Virgil jumped into the conversation and sat in the chair next to Amanda.

She spoke up for herself. "I saw his recruitment letter and decided to respond. The society had been recruiting teachers at my college in Ohio, and I decided to come for myself."

"You've been to college, dear?"

"Yes. I graduated a few weeks ago."

"My goodness. What is this world coming to? Everything all topsy-turvy. College for a Negro woman."

Amanda's ears burned. Why was the mission of education for her kind so hard to take in?

"You want to teach here?"

"Very much, ma'am." Amanda sat up straighter.

"Well, I don't see why not. I taught Sunday school before I married Mr. Milford. I taught my children in the nursery in their time. Nothing wrong with a woman schoolteacher as I can see it, Virgil."

"She say she wants the house."

"The house."

"The schoolteacher house."

Mrs. Milford shook her crown of braids. "Well, that would be hard, I'm afraid."

"I'm not sure I understand, Mrs. Milford."

"You don't have a husband, correct?"

"No. I'm unmarried."

"Well, Virgil's right. Milford Farm, I mean the town here, is a Christian town. We could not have a young woman living alone. That would not work for what we want, right, Virgil?"

"That's right, ma'am."

"No, a young woman, a pretty one such as yourself would be an attraction to all kinds of base desires, lewd behavior, and filth."

She did not want to interrupt, but felt she must speak. "I'm a Christian myself, ma'am."

"That's wonderful. But we must have propriety in all things. It's enough that folks around here aren't particularly glad that there will be a schoolhouse as it is. Folks were calling me a little crazy for doing it, but there's no harm for the Negro children to know some basics in reading, writing, and figuring. I came here from New York, and I've seen these things before."

Amanda gulped. Basics? She thought of her father's law and history books being shipped down at her expense. She had plans for so much more. Now it was all slipping away.

She felt herself slip a little further into Charles Henry's grasp. Because where else would she go? She had no other opportunity to obtain a school. She sat up a bit straighter. Sewing might help her make a living somewhere, and she could launder clothes. There wasn't much money to be made in those jobs, but it would be better than ending up in the clutches of Mr. Henry. *Please let me teach.*

Mrs. Milford, sat up, her hands folded. "I have it!"

Both she and Virgil turned to Mrs. Milford who had clasped her hands together. "Ma'am?" Virgil asked.

"The answer to this problem. We keep your schoolteacher here, she can have the house, and everything is fine."

"What's that, ma'am?" Amanda's voice sounded hollow to herself. For some reason, her heart beat furiously beneath her corset, and she wished to loosen her stays a bit, to offset the light feeling in her head.

"You need to get married, dear," Mrs. Milford explained, "as soon as possible. To Virgil. That will solve everything."

The spinning porch made no sense to her. Why didn't it stop?

Chapter Five

The thud of Miss Stewart's petite body hitting the floor made a light, hollow sound. Virgil caught her head before it hit the white plank flooring.

Marriage up? With this woman? She couldn't even sit up in the chair proper to hear what Mrs. Milford had to say.

"Mercy, her stays must be too tight. Her waist is so tiny." Mrs. Milford shook her crown of white braids back and forth.

Miss Stewart might still be slumped in his arms, but he wasn't about to do anything with her stays! Instead, he waved his large hand back and forth in front of her face. Someone once told him his hands were like palmetto fronds, and he was glad for it today. Waving them seemed to bring some air to her, and she stirred. He could smell a faint scent of orange coming from her. Instead of being embarrassed he was holding her, he felt strangely comforted.

Her black eyes snapped open, and she sat straight up, apparently mortified to see who was holding her. "I'm fine."

"Don't move too fast, dear. Best to move slow, a little at a time until the blood feeling comes back in." Mrs. Milford spoke from experience. Her fainting spells were legendary.

"I'm fine." Amanda repeated. "I need to go."

"Go where?" He helped her into the chair.

"I—I was supposed to catch the train. Wasn't I?" She had to turn to him. He could tell she didn't want to. She would rather turn to anyone else in the universe. But he was it.

Humiliation for her and him stirred in his fingertips, and he gripped his knee, to try to make the pain go away. Must have thunked it when he caught her.

"That is completely up to you, dear." Mrs. Milford's blue eyes sparkled with excitement. "Seems as if you were overcome by my proposition."

"To marry? Mr. Smithson?"

Hmm. Her voice came forward in a bit of a little girl squeak, like March when she liked something. Was that a good thing or a bad one?

"Yes, dear. Of course."

He spoke up for her. Enough of this staying quiet. "Mrs. Milford, ma'am. I wasn't looking to get married just now. Got the town to run and–"

"And you need help with the social side. Every man in charge does. What else?"

"I don't know this woman."

She waved her thin, pink hand in the air. "Who knows anyone when they get married? Goodness. You'll get to know her. March needs a mother, for heaven's sake. You been back here a year, and every young thing down in the town's been eying you. Sally would have wanted you to find a mother for March. What better mother could she have than the schoolteacher?"

Virgil sat back in his seat, trying to sift through everything Mrs. Milford said. Marriage was a serious business, especially now. And who wanted to marry him? There were some girls of eligible age in Milford, but they were all too young, younger than him and Sally. They were little sisters to him.

"How old are you?" he barked to Amanda. Didn't mean to come across so loud, but he had sacrificed his knee to her, and now he had to get married? Made no sense.

"Twenty-one." She rubbed her temples.

"The perfect age. You're not that much older, Virgil."

He kept rubbing his knee. "Who knows how old I be?"

"Don't be sassy, Virgil. See? She can marry on her own. Lovely. It's all settled then. We'll do it out here in the yard, under the tree. I just loved the slave marriages. Virgil can tell you, when he married Sally, I gave them a fine ceremony with a lovely party after."

"Except it wasn't legal."

"Excuse me?"

Sally always telling him to speak low, and about how sometimes he came across too mean and scary. He turned to Amanda, who was doing a better job of sitting up in the chair but stared at him, simply horrified at his sass. Like Sally would have been.

"Wasn't legal for Sally to marry then. She was a slave."

"Well, Virgil, I know what she was; she was my slave. And I couldn't do anything about the law. I'm just a woman for heaven's sake, I can't even vote. I just did the best that I could."

She pointed to the large, drooping tree in the yard. "There's the tree, down there. All the slave marriages take place outside. In God's cathedral. You couldn't be married in the eyes of man, but God knew what you were about. I gave Sally one of my best dresses to be married in, and she had off an entire weekend to honeymoon. Just like it was legal."

"My." One small word from Amanda, who still looked horrified.

"You say your father is gone from us. Any other family?"

"No, no ma'am." Her response was too quick. He didn't like a fast response. No thinking in it. Was Amanda telling the truth? He had a different thought about her response than when she first came here.

But was he looking to marry? In his capacity as mayor and, even more, as the preacher of the church, he needed a helpmeet. Could this high-toned city woman from up north be the one?

Shocking. Given the way he had felt about the North, he never, ever thought he would even think of marrying one of them. But here she sat, right across from him, all proper and college educated.

If they married, she would know his secret.

The thought of being revealed made his heart pound hard—in a bad way.

"You seem shocked by my idea." Mrs. Milford giggled a bit. "I have that effect sometimes. Tell you what. You both go and decide. Either put her on the train, or send a boy and tell me you want to get married and I'll get to planning. Times are hard, won't be a party like it was the first time, Virgil, but you're the mayor. We have to have something nice."

He stood and helped Amanda to her feet. Her brown pallor still didn't look quite right, and he didn't like the idea of putting her on a train just now. Still, marriage—that was a big, big step. It required thought. More than she was giving them.

"Thank you, ma'am. We let you know."

"Yes. Thank you." Amanda's voice came out less of a squeak this time, more in a monotone. He walked her to the wagon box, holding her by the elbow. She did not seem as uncomfortable with his touch as she did when he first helped her into the wagon box. Now she didn't seem to notice or care.

After he'd swung her up into the box and the horses trotted away, Amanda spoke, the words bursting out of her. "I don't want to get married."

"Well, I don't either. I will take you on to the train platform, and you can leave and we can forget this all happened."

His pride wasn't wounded. Well, maybe a little. Maybe he should look at marrying one of those young ones down in the town, once he put Amanda on the train. One of them would be fit to be a wife.

Except they were all silly and giggling and not fit to wife. At least this Miss Lady carried herself in a proper way.

But she just said she didn't want to marry. Fine by him. He didn't need to beg no one for anything. Wasn't going to start now.

They arrived at the train platform in silence. Amanda did not wait for him to help her and jumped from the wagon box, graceful and skilled, as a cat might.

She did not need his help. He escorted her to the platform, carried her bag, and put it next to her.

"Well. This it." He gestured to the train tracks.

"It is. But this doesn't feel like a solution either. Maybe we should marry."

Had the platform caved in under him? The lightness in his head must have been the same as how she felt on the veranda when she slipped to the floor. Like the rug was pulled out from under him. Now it was his turn.

"Woman, didn't you just say you didn't want to marry?"

"I'm allowed to change my mind, Mr. Smithson."

His sudden stormy countenance took her by surprise, but she was ready for him. She might be tired, staying up all night and sewing a dress for his daughter. Then, what Mrs. Milford suggested… It was so much to take in. Still, she faced him with folded arms.

"Can you be firm about something, then?"

"Very well. I can be firm since you're very hateful and mean to me for some reason. And whether or not I get on that train, you're going to be nice to me. What kind of preacher man wouldn't be nice to a woman arrived in a strange place with not a friend in the world? I don't understand what type of God you follow, but the God I know doesn't stand back and frown at people all day long."

"You speak your peace?"

"Not quite. You need to spend more time with that little girl. She loves you very much."

"I love my daughter, but she knows that. She don't need some strange Northern woman coming in to tell her strange things."

"She needs something, some female hand on her. Mrs. Milford's right. You should marry, so someone can make you see these things that you refuse to see for yourself."

"I'm not going to say things I don't mean to some Northern snip who come down here with a fancy college degree and tries to start taking over."

"When did you get the impression that I was trying to take things over?" She wrinkled her brow in confusion, and two dimples popped out on her brown cheeks, startling him.

"You, making her a dress."

"See, that's just what I mean. You need a woman in your life so you could see what that meant to her. And it helped me out at a certain time too."

A strange thing happened. He smiled. And his smile was like the bright sun breaking through the clouds on a stormy day.

Her heart went somewhere. Her heart? She needed that back. It was the only thing that she had to give, and she was going to be very careful about who to give it to.

You aren't in control of that.

The thought entered her head before she could stop it.

In the distance, the train whistle sounded, and they both turned, staring straight ahead.

This moment stretched into eternity. What did she want to do?

What did he want? Would he want to marry her? Would she want to marry him? Was there some other way for her to stay in Milford other than to marry?

Why did he dislike her so? How could they learn to get along?

Dipping her head, she prayed. *Dear God, please help me know what to do. Please protect me in this world in the work that I can do, in the good that I can do. Help me right now in this moment. In your name, amen.*

When she lifted her head, his eyes were upon her, and the stormy look in them softened, a nourishing rain in them instead.

"God speak to your heart?"

The train chose that moment to slide right up on them, making it impossible to speak above the loudness and the dark cinder-spit of the train.

The conductor slid the door open and jerked a thumb down the side of the train. "Crow car's down there. Kind of full today though. I'll collect up your money at the next station."

That settled it. There would be no crow car for her. She turned to Virgil. "I'm not getting on. I'm staying."

He waved the conductor away, who closed the door with a frown, no doubt frustrated at having to stop for no reason. Virgil led the way off of the platform. "Gotta get back to the town then. Got a wedding to plan, I see."

Shivers went up her arms at his words. A wedding. Her wedding. To this man she had not even known for two whole days. It was that or be a soiled dove to a man she had known all of her life.

Clearly, God's hand was in all of this. He had led her into this new place, this wilderness to become a new teacher, for sure, but also to become a wife and mother.

This is important work that you have tasked me to do, she prayed as she walked to the wagon. *Please, God, give me the strength and the fortitude to do it.*

The train pulled away from the platform, and the hot doors to the crow's car shut. Her shoulders squared themselves again. She did not feel sorry that she was not on the train, shuddering at the glimpse of desperate Negro humanity.

Still, when it was time to get into the wagon box and she accepted Virgil's hand, his touch struck her in a very different way. This man, this Virgil Smithson, was to be her husband. She could not be afraid to touch him now.

A pain surged in her midsection. If her father were alive, this hallmark would happen in a very different way.

Sharp, hard tears came to her eyes, and the sting of the tears mixed with the stinging of cinders as the train pulled away into the distance, taking with it one kind of life and leaving her to start another.

Tears. What was wrong with her now? Virgil turned the horses around to cross the railroad ties, very carefully, jouncing back Milford town proper.

"Why you sad?"

"I'm thinking about my father. He never will have met you."

He gripped the reins a little harder since his hands were slick with sweat. "Yeah. I'm sorry about that. Must have been a nice man."

"You saw the letter. He was very learned. He liked to take up poetry of an evening and recite. But he also believed very deeply in the poetry of the Bible. He was a man of deep faith."

"What about your mother?"

"She died when I was very young. I barely remember her. He brought me up. "

"So you say what you say about March. 'Cause you knew."

She nodded. "Yes. It was sometimes hard to tell him things. Hard to find a way. I would figure it out. He had a partner in his firm, and the partner had a wife who was helpful for some things. But that made it distant. I wanted to tell him, but I couldn't because were of the opposite sex. I often wished he would remarry, but he never did, vowing to remain true to my mother."

"Well, he loved your mamma."

"He did. I was glad of that. But I was there presently and had needs myself. There's a difference to a child."

She wrapped her arms about herself as if she were cold. Didn't have a blanket in the wagon in the summer. He wished he could help. "So the partner's lady was like a mother."

Amanda laughed, and the dimples showed in her face, bringing a kind of sun into the conversation. Her sun warmed him and made him want to snap the reins on the horse a bit, something he hadn't felt in a very long time.

"She wasn't like a mother. She was just someone I could tell things to sometimes. And given her husband…"

The sun went away. Something was wrong. "What? What about her husband?"

They were near to pulling into Pauline's yard and coming near the forge again, but he stilled the horses to hear what she had to say, 'cause everything had changed in her face. Those popped-out cute dimples went and disappeared.

"My father's partner. He had a baser purpose in mind for me. I did not like him and sought to be clear of him every chance I got. He did not believe in my education and thought it some kind of humorous game that I should attend Oberlin. My high grades earned in the Ladies' Course and some of the Gentleman's Courses proved differently. That I was capable."

She turned to him. "I came here to get away from him."

"That's what you meant when you said you didn't have a place to stay?"

"Yes. Or a friend. Charles Henry told me that my father left me without a penny. I just know that my father wouldn't have been so wasteful with his money. Not when I had no one else in the world."

"He take your things from you." A slow burn bubbled deep in his chest at the cruelty of leaving a young tiny like this all alone in the world.

"I have no way of proving anything. I've reviewed all of my father's papers. I have his diaries to review next, although I hold no hope of finding anything written down. I had to sell a good many of our things to be able to even come here."

"But you think he stole."

She nodded her head and looked down at her folded hands in her lap.

She might be a tiny, but she had spirit. Warming shame in his limbs told him he hadn't behaved right. He'd chided in her arrival in Milford, just 'cause he knew someone smart like her would find out his secret. But she'd weathered storms of her own recently, which proved the good in accepting all.

Judge not, lest ye be judged. There was powerful truth in that. Guilt seeped into his fingers, making them feel heavy. "I'm sorry your money was stolen."

"I am as well. It has happened to women of the race before. Maria Stewart, not a relation of ours, was a very famous case when her husband died and she had her living stolen from her as well. She had to write a book to be able to make her way in the world. Her book made many angry, though, and she teaches now. Her example, and the letter you sent my father, gave me the idea that I could do more, and I could do something similar for myself."

"Teaching the children?"

"Yes. I went to a lot of classes at Oberlin for my degree. But I never knew what for. The day I found that letter with the offer to come here, it was as if I understood what I was supposed to do with myself."

He clucked to the horse. "Well, you got away from evil. Still don't think a tiny like you will be able to manage some of these classes, but it's good."

"You—you think it's good I came."

"Old times mean bad times. What you just talked about sound like bad times again. Mr. Lincoln got killed, and a whole big war was fought to not have bad times anymore. So I'm glad you're down here now, so there be no Charles Henry for you. He Negro?"

"No. He's a white man."

He shook his head. Mr. Stewart sounded like a good man, but he might have done better to protect his daughter from harm. Virgil had sworn every day to protect his daughter from harm.

For true, though, the law was not designed to protect Negroes. Amanda Stewart's fate was probably cast when she was born. The sooner she understood that, the better for her.

But she was not born into slavery, so she was different. What a blessing to get education and come to help them. Her desire to help seemed to come from God. Who was he to stand in the way of what God wanted?

"I told you, people come into Milford has a hard time leaving it."

"You did say that, Mr. Smithson."

"Might have to call me Virgil now."

She hesitated. "You may call me Amanda."

"Too fancy for 'round here."

"Fancy?"

"Gotta have a quick name for everyday. What's your middle name?"

She gave a little laugh. "Aurelia."

"Even worse. Fancy name for a little bit."

"Guess I had fancy folks."

A shadow crossed her face again. Having lost a loved one, he understood her pain at the memory. Sometimes it was best not to talk about them. If she had been in his congregation, he might have touched her shoulder. Maybe embraced her in Christian comfort. Since he couldn't touch her, he said, "I'ma call you Mandy. That okay?"

"Mandy." She tested it out on her pretty shaped lips. Lips that would soon speak a wedding vow. To him. "Yes, that's fine, Virgil. I like it fine."

To hear his name on a woman's lips again—a woman who would soon be his wife?

Mighty hard to get used to, but something in him liked it fine too.

CHAPTER SIX

March broke into a dance when they pulled into Pauline's yard. Seeing the dear child's joy was worth all the waves of uncertainty doing their own dance in her stomach. When Amanda climbed down the wagon box, with Virgil's assistance, the little girl threw her arms around her and held her so tight, as if she would never let her go.

"God is so good to bring me a mamma. I prayed so hard." Then a terrified look crossed her face. "You going to be my mamma?"

A lump of emotion rose in her throat, and she rubbed the child's thin back.

"A mamma?" Pauline echoed. "Is that what's going on?"

Virgil looked at Amanda who bowed her head, unable to speak. "Mrs. Milford say if she want to stay, she have to marry."

"You?"

"Who else she marry around here?"

"I can think of some other man she might want than evil old you! Marry?" Pauline's loud tone was enough to send the entire row running from out in the field. And there it was—within minutes everyone in the small Negro town of Milford knew that their mayor was going to get married to the new schoolteacher.

"Got to get back to work, everyone," Virgil shouted above the din.

Amanda shook another woman's hand. "I don't know if they're listening to you."

"Yep, that's how it is at times."

The women surrounded her in a frenzy of plans. After they cleared out, she had more questions.

"When can I see the house and the schoolhouse?"

Virgil walked off, leaving her in the square. "We'll go when I get back. Seems like you got your hands full, talking about your dress and things."

She did. Pauline had to return to the fields, but she and March took out her only other dress, a blue and white striped one, to begin the process of cutting it down to make it suitable for a wedding. The afternoon flew by so fast that when she looked up, Virgil had returned from the smithy to take her to her new home place.

This time it was different getting into the wagon with him. She was going somewhere new, somewhere she belonged now.

"Why is your house so far away from the other citizenry?"

"Milford got plans to fill all this in between the black town and the white town of Crumpton up the road a piece. Schoolhouse and teacher's house and my house about half the way. It's not far, just a far piece to walk at the end of the day and too far for the little legs back there."

He gestured to March who sat in the back of the wagon, holding onto both sides and looking petrified.

Amanda's voice filled with concern for her soon-to-be daughter. "Are you okay, March?"

"Yes, ma'am. I just want to get on home is all."

"We'll be there soon."

She focused ahead. The wagon climbed a rise in the hill, with buildings perched on the right side of the road. The surroundings were so pleasant, a healing balm of warmth soothed away the pain in her midsection, the pain that came about at the loss of her father.

The view of the slightly unfinished schoolhouse was all new pine, but the house next to it, Virgil's house, was edged in brick. Much more sophisticated than she had a right to expect, the graceful brick house dazzled her. She and her father had lived out of boardinghouses in Oberlin all of her life, carrying crates of books between places.

This was to be her home.

"Schoolhouse not done yet. When you want to start school?"

"Monday, please." She barely wanted to wait until then, since there was so much work to do to help the people.

"It's a harvesting time of year, so folks might not come as they should, but you have a good idea not to put things off. But you need time to get things ready. I need some time to finish it. Better start the next Monday."

"That's fine."

"We finish it up tomorrow probably. Wedding probably be next Saturday, and we'll have a church service here at the finished schoolhouse on Sunday and school the next Monday. Good enough."

Her heart thudded at the thought of being a married woman in just a few days. Would her father even know her if he were still here?

Virgil came around to help her out of the wagon, and she did not feel a jolt at his touch as she had before. Instead, his deep voice and discussions of how things would proceed soothed her.

The order of things was a relief to her—a life she knew how to live. And such a change from the previous twenty-four hours when everything appeared to be in complete tumult.

She approached the schoolhouse and entered, taking in the heady scent of pine and newness all throughout with desks that shone. Some of the edges on the walls needed smoothing.

"Church will be in here too. For now." Virgil came up behind her and stood.

"So, in effect," she said, caressing the lectern up front, "we would have been sharing this space anyway."

Virgil coughed and seemed a bit uncomfortable. She bit the inside of her cheek to keep from smiling. Was it possible that she had stirred the gentleman?

"I was looking to share it with a male schoolteacher. It was going to be different…"

"Of course. What about the teacher house?" She referred to the living quarters built and attached onto the schoolhouse, where the schoolteacher was supposed to live. She smiled as March came running back into the schoolroom from the specially built teacher house.

"Yes. You welcome to stay there until the wedding. Good to have a choice now about where you stay."

"There's not more than one room in your house?"

"There is."

"Well, couldn't I stay in the guest room in your house?" She folded her arms for protection.

He coughed again. "I don't rightly know about that."

"We'll be married in two days. I don't see what difference it makes then."

"I'm the preacher here. It matters."

"No one else is out here but us."

"It matters. I know."

She stepped up and stared him in the face, unafraid. He certainly could be obstinate when he wanted. "What will this marriage be like?"

"I don't get your meaning."

She ran her hands over one another, wishing she had gloves on them. "Am I to be your wife in all things, Mr. Smithson?"

" Call me Virgil. And we don't need to discuss that just now."

"Why not? We're alone here."

He seemed to have forgotten that and looked all around him. "Best be time to leave then."

"I think we should have an understanding."

"Fine. It's up to you."

"Me?"

"Yes. Womenfolk are the ones who determine these things."

"I see. And you have no say in it?"

"Didn't say that. I just say women determine things. You always twisting my words."

"I don't mean to offend. I just want to know what I may expect."

"You can expect to be Mrs. Smithson. Teach the school, be March's mamma, Mrs. Mayor, and the preacher's wife. Got enough to handle there, seems like."

She stroked her gloveless hands. Yes. Virgil spoke a full plate just then, with the exception of the garnish on the meal or the dessert.

Children.

She could not say what she meant any further, since she had already pressed her point. She would have to wait until after they were married.

March would be her daughter, but would there be any others? Ever? She turned and walked out the door and made her way to Virgil's brick house just up the road. Could she live a life without the expectation most women had?

Help me, God.

She always, always had to find these things out the hard way.

Mandy carried herself a bit too bold for his taste. Or maybe it was that she seemed spicy after seeing a lifetime of submissive women in servitude. She was different, new, thrilling in that respect. How would he adjust?

Virgil knew what she was trying to say. But he meant what he said too. It was up to her. Every time she looked at him, he still felt inadequate somehow, as if he didn't measure up to her standard.

Even though he had a successful smithy shop folks frequented from miles around.

Even though he was the mayor of this small town.

Even though he was a preacher man.

Still, he didn't quite measure up in her eyes. Because if she ever knew his secret, she would reject him completely.

And she would find out because she had high college education.

She would hate him once she knew.

Dear God, is it wrong of me to marry this woman without telling her? Should she know before we marry?

"Oohhh." A croon of pleasure escaped her as he opened the door to the house he'd built for himself and March. "This is beautiful, Virgil, just beautiful. You built this yourself?"

She walked around, admiring his handiwork, letting her hand travel over the smoothed pine furniture and the carved fireplace, but the overstuffed red velvet davenport in the middle of the room seemed to impress her.

"You need a few rugs, but I can get those made. Better yet, I can teach this young lady how." Amanda's small hand went to the top of March's braids as she sidled up next to her after his daugther's wanderings. His child smiled under her regard.

"I tried to keep it all nice."

"It's a very nice house."

"Got its own kitchen. It's part of the house."

"Amazing. I look forward to cooking there. Let me see the bedrooms." She walked upstairs to where they were.

Her feet made creaking noises in the floorboards. She walked all around, approving of everything with feminine ohhs, ahhs, and cooing. He stared into the empty coals. He supposed he did well enough to earn her approval, but he dreaded her disapproval, feeling his stomach grow hard as he thought about it.

He spoke, hoping to chase his thoughts away. "I buy a cook-stove now, since you here."

Mandy and March came down the stairs, and Mandy's eyes shone with happiness. "I can deal with the fireplace for now. Very satisfactory indeed. I should be proud to live here. Are you going to see to similar improvements for the town?"

His eyes met hers. Was her mind so quick she knew his heart—his dream for Milford? "I had thought that. We do well enough on the crops, we could work to change out people's cabins for stronger houses."

"Oh, Virgil. I think that is a wonderful plan. No wonder you're the mayor."

"I just have to find the time."

"We'll figure it out." She looked embarrassed. "I mean, you will. This is truly something. And the church someday?"

"Someday." Virgil looked off in the distance. "That's my biggest dream of all."

"We'll pray about it."

His heart lurched at her set, determined face. What would her disgust for him look like? Would she even want to have children with him when she found out? Was that even a possibility for them?

She took off her bonnet and set it on the main table in the center of the room. She approached him and laid a hand on his arm. "What you have done here, sir, is an accomplishment. I've seen houses as fine in Ohio, and I think it is a wonderful thing that you seek to help the people in Milford."

He bowed his head. "Thank you."

"Thank you, Mr. Smithson. Virgil. If you have provisions in the pantry, I can fix us some dinner."

She removed her hand from his arm, and the spot where her slight, light hand had rested fairly glowed. Or it felt as if it did.

"I—March can show you where everything is."

"Of course."

She walked away into the kitchen, almost smiling.

Who knew or understood the ways of a woman? She disapproved of him as recently as this morning, yelled at him at the train depot, but now thought his work very fine.

She won't think you so fine, when she knows you can't read and write.

He gripped the mantel, facing the fireplace. He could not let himself get invested again. Loving a woman had nearly taken him under before. He could not let it happen again. There was March to think about.

Amanda Stewart had to be stopped, and the next time she touched his arm with her slight hand, he would remove it.

God, give me strength to do what I have to, to distance her from me.

He hoped God heard him.

Virgil Smithson had the makings to be a great man. Could that be her purpose, to help him to that task?

If only he liked her a little more. Maybe it was her clothing that offended him. She would try her best to look nice on their wedding day so he wouldn't feel as if he'd been cheated.

"What does your father like to eat?"

"Bacon and grits, I guess." March shrugged her shoulders. "But that's not dinner."

She opened the pantry door and pulled out some salt fish. She could make a gravy with that and have porridge. Making over a dress would take most of tomorrow, but at some point, they would have to stock up on provisions.

Amanda showed March how to soak the fish until it was soft and made a savory gravy out of it. There was enough flour to make a quick loaf of light bread, and soon she had March working through the dough. She rolled it into balls so they would cook faster. The air soon filled with the yeasty smells of baking bread from the Dutch oven in the fireplace.

When she set dinner before him, he prayed over it and made short work of the food on his plate.

"Was it okay?" she asked.

"Fine. Filled the belly and the soul. I'm going out to take care of the animals."

"When you come back in, I would like to read a Bible verse."

A strange look crossed his face, but he said nothing as he went outside. She and March made short work of cleaning up the kitchen and sat, waiting for him to return.

Once he did, she held out her father's Bible to him.

"Getting late, and I'm tired. Big day today. Let's just pray."

She felt a bit rejected, but nodded. They sat on the overstuffed davenport and held hands in a circle.

"Father God, please bless us as we go into this new part of our lives. Help March to be a well-behaved child and learn her lessons and walk in your light. Help Mandy, Lord, as she starts on a new path to serve in your spirit with honor and truth." *And help me, Lord, to be the man you would have me be in all things.* "Amen."

He let go of her hand as if it were a hot coal. "March, you go on up to bed with Miss Mandy. Good night now."

He stayed sitting as they stood. March, as she usually was at night, complied and went to bed quickly. Mandy returned to his side.

Virgil nodded in the direction of the teacher's house. "It's probably best you go stay next door. Like I said. I don't want folks getting the wrong impression."

"I can get to breakfast and things much faster if I'm here."

"Good night, Miss Mandy. I mean Mandy. It's late and I'm going to turn in." Virgil stepped around her and went upstairs.

Well. A hard man to get to know. She rearranged her skirts and sat on the overstuffed red davenport. She would do her best to get to know him and to meet his expectations in all things.

The same way she tried to do with God.

Upstairs, Virgil could not sleep. Mandy had not left. She was still downstairs, sleeping—or trying to sleep—on that narrow davenport. How comfortable would she be?

She hadn't gotten good sleep last night, sewing that dress up for March. Probably didn't have any good sleep, coming down to Georgia to teach in Milford.

She at least deserved to be comfortable.

He went downstairs and craned his head into the living area to see her. Sure enough, she had lain down on the davenport. Made those cute little snoring sounds like she'd made before. He put one of Sally's quilts on her, hoping she had at least been able to loosen her stays.

He reminded himself. Her stays weren't none of his concern.

Back in bed again, he thought about how in a few days, it would be her wifely duty to lie here beside him in the four-poster bed he had hewn when he came back last year after the war.

Was that why he had made it so big? To have a wife in it?

Mrs. Milford had a point. Someone like him did need a wife.

Did he need one in that way? Would he require that Mandy be a wife in all ways, as she'd said?

He couldn't face her hatred of him. Better that she look at him as she had today, as someone who was capable and would protect her.

Since that's what she deserved.

His teeth gnashed in fresh horror at the thought of that white man up in Ohio thinking that Mandy was only suitable to be his mistress. Couldn't he see how fine and genteel she was?

She could do anything. Remade March a dress from her own, made a fine meal. God had formed her to be a man's treasure, not a man's sin. Who was this man who took what belonged to her?

If I knew how to read, I could find out.

He turned over and punched the pillow, ignoring the same sinking feeling in his stomach when he thought about reading. Thought about Mandy holding out her father's Bible to him to read from—a trusted part of her life, he could tell.

He had tried to learn how to read. When he had bought his freedom, the law forced him to leave Georgia and he wandered all over, smithing on the road, and had paid many a person to teach him. But it was too hard. He just wasn't smart enough to learn.

Too old now anyhow. Reading was for children. It would be good for March to learn, as her mother had wanted, and for her to learn how to be a good wife and mother.

Or a teacher. What an idea, that March could be a teacher. Mandy was one.

This world was changing, in a lot of ways for the good, but in a lot of ways, the rapid change unsettled. He'd better learn how to adapt with it.

Now with a wife by his side, he could rise high, and the possibilities seemed vast and open.

If only she didn't despise him after learning everything about him.

Chapter Seven

The morning of Amanda's wedding day dawned bright and hot.

She sat up on the small davenport and stretched herself out. All yesterday, Virgil had worked and made preparations at the Milford plantation. She had been consumed with reworking her blue and white striped dress into something more appropriate, with less volume and cloth.

Yesterday she'd had the pleasure of meeting more of Milford's citizens, people whom she would be living, working, and staying with for the rest of her life.

Because that's what marriage was, a lifelong proposition.

The decision had been made, almost for her, to yoke herself in harness with a man she barely even knew. Who was Virgil Smithson? Would he be kind to her? There were other possibilities, and cold climbed up her arms as she thought about how some men were to their wives.

She hoped for kindness. Her father had only ever shown her kindness. At the thought of him, the pain at his loss came afresh, and tears started in the corner of her eyes again.

Please, God, please protect me in this new world, in this new circumstance. And please, Daddy, look out for me. Help me to learn to be a good wife and a good mother to March. Who stood there watching her, tears in the corners of her own eyes.

Amanda sniffled. "What're you doing watching me, child?"

"I see you sad, crying on your wedding day. Mrs. Milford say you start out a day that way, it will always be that way, so I crying too."

She reached out an arm to the thin girl and pulled her in close. "No. I'm not planning on crying all of the time, honey. I was thinking about my papa and I was sad he won't see me getting married."

"What was your papa like? Was he like mine?"

No. "My papa went to school and studied for a long time. He wanted to figure out how to use the law of the land to show people that slavery was wrong. He was called an abolitionist, meaning someone who wanted for the wrong to be gone. And he got to see the fulfillment of his work come to pass, so he was successful too. His lungs were never very strong, though, and that's how he died. Just a few weeks ago."

"Seem like my mamma died just a few months ago too."

She squeezed the girl a little tighter, feeling the thin shoulder blades beneath March's nightdress. "Tell me something about her."

March turned to her with a frown on her face. "Papa says I mustn't. Says I should forget all about her."

It was her turn to frown. "Why's that?"

"She's dead and nothing, nothing will bring her back."

"I didn't ask to bring her back, child. Just something you remember about her. Memories is what keeps the people we love close. There isn't any wrong in that."

"Still, I have to listen to what Papa say. You said it too."

"I did?" She pointed toward her chest. "I don't recall ever being that provincial."

"You said honor thy father and thy mother. Just the other day."

March's mind kept things like a trap. She would do well in school. "I did say that. So I suppose that you keep silent about your mother, just like everyone else around here."

"I going to go wash my face to get ready to be up under the wedding tree." She galloped her little body out into the bright sunshine.

How could this be? Did people get erased in this place once they died? She donned a robe and stood up. How terrible it would be to come south from everything she had been through, just to disappear. Yet, it used to happen all the time and was one reason why her father had been so protective. People had even been kidnapped and carried off to be enslaved. Like Solomon Northrup. He himself had said enslavement was an extreme difficulty, but doubly so for women.

If she were stolen away and sold into slavery, it would be a terrible thing for her, she had come to understand. So, her father's goal, even when she'd been very young, was to make her visible and not easy to hide away.

Soon, I will be Mrs. Virgil Smithson, rendered invisible again. For my own protection.

Still, if she had the protection of a man like Virgil, she would not fall into the clutches of Charles Henry.

She made her way around to the kitchen in bare feet, turned to get a plate off of the table and smacked herself hard into Virgil's hard, broad chest. She drew a deep breath in. "Oh. My. I apologize."

She backed away. He stood there, peering at her with that stormy look again. Would he wear that look when they stood before the Crumpton church preacher, brought in specially for them to marry? Why did he have to appear as if he were getting the shabby end of the deal?

"Got to watch where you're going, Mandy."

"Yes. Just trying to get some breakfast together before we have to be at the place." Why couldn't she call it the wedding tree? That's what Mrs. Milford called it. The place where she would let her slaves "marry" one another.

Except her marriage would be real and legal.

"Make it quick."

"You don't want something nice for today?"

"Didn't say that. I just…"

All of a sudden he seemed exasperated with her. What had she done?

A thought popped into her mind and burst through her lips. "Were you angry at what I said to March just now?"

He scowled at her. "I don't know what you are talking about."

She took some ham steaks out of the cupboard. She could make a gravy to go with the grits. Virgil had said he had no chickens but hoped to start a flock. She'd be eager to have eggs and chicken soon enough.

"I asked her to tell me something about her mother, and she said you told her not to mention her anymore."

"No need for calling up the dead."

"Maybe March has a need. Did you think of that?" She sliced the ham. Red eye gravy was best made in small bits. She lit the wood in the newly purchased cookstove to boil water for coffee. "Just because someone is gone doesn't mean you can't remember them to love them."

"She is a child, not grown like you what lost your father. She need to get on and do what she need to for her life."

"All the more reason to remember her mother." She faced him, or more likely, faced off with him. "I don't want to fuss about this. I didn't ask you about Sally because I knew how you would be about it. I just feel left out somehow. I just get bits and pieces."

"You have got to be one of the strangest women anybody know 'round here. Somebody dies. There ain't no need in talking about them. They gone." He pulled up his suspender straps. "Got to water the livestock."

He left through the side door as March came in with a pitcher of water.

Once again, she'd succeeded in stirring up the fire between them, this time about Sally. Would she never learn? It was always best to keep the coals banked. She would have to lead a banked-coal existence from now on.

Except that was not who she was. Would she have to change her ways and be more like a slave?

No. Slavery was over. They would have to learn how to find their voices. That's what she would teach them to do. Starting on Monday. But first, she had to be married.

Miss Mandy was someone who would talk him right into an early grave. Just like someone from up north, always asking questions, poking into things that weren't her concern. He watered down his horses, patting their rumps. "Sometimes best to just leave things be, " he said aloud to them.

One of those things best left alone was Sally. Yet he couldn't help but think of her, strangely enough, here on his second wedding day.

Well, no. His real wedding day. His first real one.

The wedding with Sally was just a play ceremony with a big party with Mrs. Milford. An excuse to have cake and lemonade for her "People.". No, the marriage to Mandy would be real, and he had to do right by her and protect her, from now into forever.

Scary sounding, but as a man who had seen something of the world and not the thin scared boy he'd been seven years ago, chased from Milford, he knew more of what he could handle and what he couldn't. He would handle Miss Mandy and her curiosity. As her husband, she would have to trust him in all things.

He scraped the last of the grits and red eye gravy into his mouth and swilled down his coffee. "I be at work, be back to get you later. You okay?"

"I'm fine here with March. I'll see you later."

He pushed a hat onto his head and walked out to the wagon. That was a better attitude. One that would take her farther than the other. It would take some time to have her learn, to gentle her, but Mandy was smart enough. Didn't she have one of them college degrees?

There were two weddings he didn't have to conduct in his capacity as Milford's Negro preacher. One was his wedding to Sally. The other was his wedding to Mandy.

Today's wedding loomed large in his mind, and he recalled his wedding to Sally eight years ago.

Sally was Mrs. Milford's favorite maid and, as such, was entitled to all of the wonders of a wedding. She loaned Sally a white dress and made sure there was a wreath of orange blossoms to weave into her hair.

He had been so nervous, but Sally had looked to him to take the lead. He was the one in charge. When they joined hands and Mr. Milford spoke the words over them since no preacher was required, they were man and wife in the eyes of the Milford farm community. No where else.

This marriage to Mandy would go on record at the Franklin County courthouse and would be recognized wherever they went.

Before, Mrs. Milford had thrown a big reception with cake and lemonade for all of the slaves. This time, it was up to them to provide their own reception of ginger water and teacakes. This time Reverend Arnold would speak the words. Reverend Arnold minded a great bit, since he didn't like marrying Negroes, but it couldn't be helped. He certainly couldn't do it.

He made sure his brown summer broadcloth was brushed and ready to wear. Was March ready? What about Mandy herself?

He moseyed out of the house to care for the horses. Out of the corner of his eye, March appeared, her neat braids pinned to her head for a change. "You look nice there, little bit."

"Thank you, Papa. So do you."

March danced around, as she loved to do, until her fidgeting rattled him. Where was Mandy?

He almost grew tired of waiting when Mandy came forward from the house. He stood to meet her. The length and cut of her dress was different. She'd slimmed it down considerably, and the blue and white stripe flattered her beautiful, smooth red-brown skin. Her edge of her neatly coiled hair peeked out from underneath her bonnet.

"I'm here. Sorry to be late."

"I see. Let me help you up to the wagon box."

She lightly touched his hand as he helped her up, and her soft hand was as nice as anything he had ever felt before.

March scrambled onto the wagon tongue. Virgil climbed up the side, and they started off.

"Everyone gets married beneath the tree?"

"It's a custom. We don't have a church just yet. So the tree in front is a nice space to have the wedding, and then you can have a picnic on the grounds."

"Also helps Mrs. Milford to not have Negro company in her parlor."

"You got that, hmm."

"I was not raised in slavery, Virgil, but I understand the prejudices that caused it to continue."

"She done a lot for us. Some folks around here think she's crazy. She from up north like you."

"And there is still more to be done. At least her Northern heritage allows her to recognize that it's a new world." Mandy turned to him. "She has a great regard for you."

"Guess so."

A smile played about Mandy's lips.

"What are you thinking?"

"I think if Mrs. Milford were a good deal younger and a Negress, she would wish to be under the tree with you."

"Come on, Mandy. That kind of thing's not spoken of 'round here."

She searched the road around them. No one was about, but it could be hard to tell sometimes.

"It's not hard to believe," she finally said. "Even if you seek to have a stern manner, you cut a fine figure. You have a certain way that you look that is pleasing to the female eye."

"Mandy—" He cleared his throat, scarcely able to believe what he was about to say. "You saying you like the way I look?"

"My goodness, Virgil." She gave a giggle. "I think I was saying that Mrs. Milford likes the way you look."

He took his hands off of the reins to lay a finger of warning on his lips. "Mandy."

"But I'm not completely opposed to you either. You'll pass muster."

"Thank you. Hard to tell with you talking all that teacher talk what you saying."

"I don't quite get what you are saying, sir."

"I'm saying, you Northern folk got to have everything all prettied up and gussied up for show. Down here, it's hot and we don't want everything dressed up for show. Just come forward and speak it plain."

"And what would you say, Mr. Smithson? I mean, Virgil."

"What I'm saying about you, Mandy?"

"A woman likes to hear something nice on her wedding day."

The road dust clogged his throat something powerful today. Good thing they were coming up on the Milford house where he could get a swallow of lemonade.

"Hmm. Well then. You look mighty fine."

The brightness went away from her face. Her voice was quiet. "Thank you."

Her frown reflected disappointment. Did she expect more? He wished he could be more eloquent when he spoke to her, but he couldn't. He just got all tongue-tied around her, in a way he never was with other women.

Well, she would have to get used to him. She'd be a blacksmith's wife. If she wanted someone grand, she should have stayed up there in Ohio and found him.

He stopped in front of the Milford house where it seemed as if the entire hamlet had turned out to see him be married. They'd really come for the teacakes, but it still brought a lump to his throat to see them all there.

After he tied up the horses, he came around to the side, after March had scrambled out of the back of the wagon. He reached up to help Mandy down from the wagon box.

The truth hit him, hard, as a blow to the head. They were all here to see her. The entire gathering of this wedding was about Amanda Stewart.

Some folks started to clap. He held his hand out to Mandy, and someone yelled, "Grab her on out."

A bride should not have to jump down, so he took his hands and put them around her waist and lifted her out instead. His nerves made him clumsy in handling her, and she got pushed up against him. Sweat trickled down his back as if he were still at the forge. He hadn't been so close to a woman in many years.

When her feet touched the ground, the entire gathering burst into applause. Mandy pushed her bonnet back, and Mrs. Milford made tiny silly claps with her hands and smiled. "I just love a romance."

Romance? He barely even knew this woman. Still, looking at the way his town had gathered to meet their Mrs. Mayor, he got an inkling that he better get to know her, sooner, rather than later. These folks wouldn't stand for him to treat her poorly.

He felt the exact same way.

Was her face heated? When she pushed back from Virgil, she adjusted her bonnet to hide her burning cheeks so no one could see her embarrassment at their collision. She had never been pushed against a man's body before. Well, not in public anyway. And this wasn't any man—he would be her husband in short order.

Peering out from the bonnet, she bore witness to many smiling friendly faces, with the exception of a man who stood beside Mrs. Milford. She pushed the bonnet back and stared at the gathered crowd. They all cheered.

The cheering made her feel so much better, buoyed up on a wave of support from strangers she didn't even know. Lawrence Stewart's only child might not fare so bad in this world. Maybe people wanted some time free from their responsibilities, but from what she could see, they were all there to see Virgil's new bride, to see if she measured up.

March gave her a bouquet of roses and a wreath meant for her hair. Amanda set her bonnet in the wagon and snuggled the orange blossoms onto her hair. Ideally, her hair should be out and free of her braids, but she'd decided to keep it braided since she had so much hair pinned onto her head.

"I haven't had a slave wedding in years," Mrs. Milford said. "Except this one is all legal. So nice for you."

Amanda hadn't been a slave, but she didn't stop to correct Mrs. Milford, still a little overwhelmed by the people. "Thank you."

"Best of luck to you. You're getting a good man in Virgil."

"Thank you."

"Let's go," Virgil grunted.

"Slow down, Mr. Smithson. Can't people enjoy a good time?"

"Thought I told you to call me Virgil."

"I apologize."

He held out a hand and she grabbed it. This time his broad fingertips were cold. She looked up at him. Faint beads of sweat lined his forehead.

Well, she supposed it wasn't every day a man was coerced into marrying a stranger. When they'd left the house, she'd wrapped March's flowers in a hanky embroidered by her mother. Unwrap ping the flowers from it, she offered him the hanky and Virgil used it.

Several nearby chuckled. Virgil gave a slight smile. "Hot day."

"Sure enough," someone yelled out. "You be fine, Mr. Mayor. You got a prize with you for sure."

The sour-faced white man next to Mrs. Milford spoke up. "Let's get this over with."

So this was Reverend Arnold, Mrs. Milford's minister of note. She told him, "Oh, of course, Reverend. You have your sermon to write for tomorrow, don't you?"

"Among other things."

Paired together, the reverend escorted Mrs. Milford to the tree, and the crowd parted to let them through. Amanda and Virgil followed amidst a loud chorus of cheering and whistling. She couldn't hear much of what they were saying, but she gathered that several of the comments were of a more raucous nature. Virgil would need the hanky to stay free of sweat. She wished for one herself.

When they reached the tree, Reverend Scarpes held up his hands, "Quiet, all of you. It's time to speak the words of the ceremony. We have to make sure these two give proper responses or it won't be legal."

The crowd became very silent.

It was shocking that the words they spoke took such a short time yet had such importance. When it came time for the ring, Virgil pulled from his pocket something very unique and different, a ring fashioned of iron, one he'd made himself. It was a bit too big, however, and she had to keep pushing the smooth wide band back with her thumb.

"All right. Now, I declare that by the state of Georgia these two are legally and officially married." The reverend folded his hands and looked back at them both. "You going to kiss her?"

A dull thrum beat steadily in her ears. Virgil turned to her, regarding her as if she were some new thing he didn't know what to do with. "All that kissing ain't called for," he said, his voice stormy.

Something inside of Amanda withered away.

Someone shouted, "I'll kiss her, Virg. If you don't want to!"

People burst into laughter. Sharp, hot, tears rose up in Amanda's eyes. *Don't shed. Not a one.* It wouldn't do to show her pain and hurt. What would it get her? Virgil was right; she was here to teach school. That's all. No kissing involved.

Before she knew it, he bent close and applied his lips, which felt softer than she had expected, to her forehead. He took his time pulling away and whispered, "I pray you know what you doing, Mrs. Smithson."

The crowd cheered and pressed forward, separating them from one another, hugging them. But Amanda considered that the first words spoken to her by her new husband were an admonition and a warning.

A kiss to the forehead. She must be the ugliest woman in the world.

Chapter Eight

"You can't keep sleeping on that davenport. There's an upstairs bedroom, and I can fashion you a bedstead out of rope ties. "

The celebration was over, and they'd arrived at their home, a sleeping March in tow. Virgil hadn't spoken until they were on the ground, next to the wagon, afraid to stir March. The real reason he hesitated had to do with not wanting to go into the house with her. Together. As a married couple. Legally.

"I—I guess not."

He stepped away from her. "I'm not looking to force you to nothing."

"I appreciate that." More of that snip in her voice came out.

Virgil tried to smooth things over. "We just got thrown into this, but I'm going to see it through."

"If you're going to do that, you might as well do it with some cheer."

The tone in her voice surprised him. "I don't get your meaning."

"Like today. At the tree."

"Excuse me?"

"When you said there was no need for that kissing stuff."

He let the reins drop to the ground. This woman never stopped interfering. "Well, it was true. I wasn't saying nothing to you that you didn't know."

"You're a preacher. You've performed all of those marriage ceremonies for the slaves." "They weren't legal, lot of them."

"They are now. How many times did the bride and groom not kiss at the end?"

Well, now. That was something to think about, he had to admit. Nothing came to him.

"That's what I thought. Once. Today."

He led the horses to the stake in front of the house. He should have taken them to the barn. Why was he trying to explain himself to this tiny instead of taking care of his livestock? "I kissed you."

"As if I were March."

"You, like March, are in my protection, and you young." He spoke the words a little loudly, because those words helped him keep her separate from everything else in his life.

"So that's how it's going to be."

"I told you, it would be how you wanted it to be."

"And what if I said that I wanted a kiss in front of the tree, a real kiss, like every other bride should get on her wedding day?"

Bless it if she didn't start sniffling and everything. Who knew what a woman thought? How could he tell?

"Look, I didn't want to presume. Mandy, we barely know each other. What if I had grabbed you up and started kissing on you and you didn't want that? I might have been humiliated in front of the town."

"So instead you humiliated me."

Lord, that woman had a way with words.

"I'm sorry if you were humiliated. I didn't mean to. I just didn't know what you wanted."

"Guess I'll have to be more straightforward about it from now on."

"I guess so." He untied the horses from the stake, glad that was all resolved.

"Stay here a minute." She took the reins, the smoothness of her palm stirring him. She tied up the horses again, then faced him, fists on her hips. "Do it now."

"Do what?"

"Kiss me. As you should have at the wedding tree."

"Before God, Mandy, I can't kiss you now."

"Can't or won't?"

"I don't know."

"I said what I wanted."

He grasped her forearms, ignoring the jolt in their connection that caused the hair on his arms to stand on end. "Maybe you done this before, you so bold and all."

"Is that what matters to you now?"

"No, you just surprise me."

"Kiss me." She put forward her chin, and her pretty lips followed.

In spite of himself, in spite of what he knew would be better protection for her, he bent down to meet to her sweet lips. Except he didn't make it. A giggle rose from the back of the wagon. March.

He pulled back instantly, a wave of shame washing over him. Why was he carrying on so in front of his daughter?

He set Mandy from him in the gentlest way and untied the reins. "Now you see what you did? She's awake."

The look on Mandy's face was one of disappointment, either at March being awake or him not kissing her.

She turned to the little girl, lifting her out of the wagon with tenderness. Her words came gently. "It's late and time for bed, March."

"Listen to your new mamma. Best take her in. I'll take care of the horses."

Mandy swept past him. The maddening, teasing scent of orange oil and horses mingled in his nose, and his heart sank. He already was a disappointment to her. And to himself. What kind of harm would it have done to kiss her?

Her kiss would pull him into a pit of fiery hell he wouldn't begin to know how to climb out of. He couldn't let that happen again. He had too much to do.

Sundays were a day when she typically felt peace, but not on this Sunday. This time, when she woke, she woke as a wife. On a bedstead. In a room by herself. The wide, cool, iron band that encircled her finger reminded her she was a wife in name only.

She made quick work of her morning's ablutions so she could prepare breakfast, made easier with Virgil's fashioning of a cookstove.

Virgil had warned her that folks would be coming from miles around to attend service. He didn't have service every Sunday, but twice a month instead. Why just twice a month? People needed to hear God's word more often than that. But if she couldn't even convince Virgil to kiss her…

She mixed up griddle cakes and fried bacon, drawing March out of bed and to her side. She planted a quick kiss amongst March's braids. "Get your face washed and get dressed."

"I just love griddle cakes, Mamma. Haven't had none in the longest time. Worth eating, anyway. Thanks for making them."

Warmth cascaded through Amanda at the child's ease in using the name. "You're welcome, child. Go on and get ready."

As Amanda stirred the leftover batter, a shadow fell in the room. She looked up. Virgil stood there, his feet bare and in his shirtsleeves.

She shouldn't be embarrassed, but she was. This man was her husband and she had never seen his bare feet before.

"Morning," Virgil said.

"Good morning."

Silence between them. She had no idea what to do except keep working.

"Sleep well?"

"Well enough, thank you."

"When we go to town next, we get you some material for dresses if you like."

"Thank you for that. I prefer my mourning for now. I want people to know what a fine man my father was."

"Didn't say he wasn't. Raised him up a fine daughter, didn't he? I just want you to be more comfortable."

"Since I'm here now?"

"Yes."

March came running back in, and they ate their griddle cakes with March chirping all about how school the next day was going to be an event.

"I heard tell, Papa that people want to stay over, so's they can be here for schooling the next morning."

His handsome face carried the stormy look again. He stroked his neatly trimmed beard. "Might need more than one schoolteacher."

"Can't marry two wives, lest you be a follower of Joseph Smith."

His brows met in the center of his forehead. "Got me a wife now. There's no need of more, but it may be worth the while to put the teacher advertisement forward again."

"Or I can make inquiries at Oberlin."

"Would you visit there?"

She chewed on her bacon thoughtfully. "I might. I just got here, but it may be that I can figure out that business with my papa. It wouldn't be until autumn anyway."

"I wouldn't want you to go alone."

"Thank you. Let's see how the school gets going down here, and then we'll make the appropriate inquiries. It's good to see so many want an education."

"Gotta make sure you educating on the right things."

She looked up at him. "I'm sure my training has prepared me well."

"Not talking about your training. I'm talking about what the people need. To learn how to be Christian. Have good morals. Now that the old time is gone, people start acting wrong, wanting to drink and carry on. It's not good for them."

"You speak as if I'm teaching beyond the children."

He laughed. "I'm sure of it. Might have two sessions, one in the morning time, and one at night for those in the fields. I know Pauline and Isaac been talking about learning how to read."

"I'll teach her, Papa. I might be a school teacher myself someday. Just like Miss Mandy. I mean, my mamma."

March slipped her thin frame in the chair next to Amanda, and she hugged her new daughter. "Let me finish eating, and I'll change out your hair ribbons."

"No need a doing that. She can do for herself."

"I'm her mamma now. I want to change out her hair ribbons."

He bowed his head to his plate and said nothing more. Why was it so hard for him to let her do such a little thing to help? That's what she was there for. What good would she be if she didn't help do the little things, like make March look nice for Sunday services?

He surely looked nice. His black broadcloth and shirt were neat, as any other day that he wore them. His beard and moustache were low on his face, and, as they finished breakfast, he donned a round black derby. They walked to the little building that housed the school and church and opened the doors. March took a large metallic bell to the door and shook it as loudly as she could. The summoning bell—something Amanda would be expected to use the next day. March could help her.

In about thirty minutes, the small church building was crowded full of people. Yes, she would have to encourage him to have services more often. Not only were the people of Milford hungry for knowledge, they hungered for spiritual food as well. Before services started, she offered him her father's Bible, and he held it close, the sight warmed her like a blanket surrounded her.

However, his hat had left a ring around his hair. That's something she should have attended to as his wife, and it made her feel a bit uncomfortable as he stood up and spoke. She needed to do a better job of keeping track of him as she went about her day.

"I'm speaking from Daniel today. That's the lesson I'm putting to you."

He had the Bible in his hands, but he did not open it or stay near it as he spoke. He wandered over the front part of the room—far away from the text. Why?

She opened her Bible, the one that had been her mother's and listened to him say, "Daniel chapter three, the children of the fiery furnace. They had faith. Old king asked them to bow down and worship a false god. An idol. This is where you have a whole lot of danger in your life. When someone come along, don't matter how good they look, or what they say in their mouth with a silver tongue. You got to be aware they are trying to get you—like that old king, Nebuchadnezzar. He thought he could get them with a pretty thing. People try to shine pretty things in front of you, and you got to rise up and say no to all of that. Don't need no shiny things."

"Amen!" The crowd roared. Their approval nearly made her jump from her skin.

"You can't give in. You got to show them there's only one way to get to your heart. God's way. Children in the furnace say no too. Guess what happened?"

"Tell it, Brother!"

"He threatened to throw them into that fiery furnace."

"Oh no!"

"Yes." Laughter broke out at Virgil's insistence. "He say, put the children—Meshach, Shadrach and Abednego—put them in the furnace."

"They thought they was going to die!" someone cried out, caught up in Virgil's rhetoric. Amanda shook her head. Amazing how he could move people.

"Sure did! But what did my God do?"

"Praise him!"

"What did he do? How he do? They went to burn those children. And it didn't work! See, God rewards the faithful. You got to have faith. You got faith in God and what he will do—it don't matter what no king do. It don't matter what shiny thing he put in front of you. It don't matter what the government say or the landlord."

"Praise him!"

"You all right with God, he going to see to you, protect you through the fiery furnace, just as he did those children! That's what he will do for you!"

Every hair on her body stood on end.

She had never seen anything like the way Virgil preached. He stood up there, his eyes alight, gesturing, waving, insisting. The people in the congregation urged him on and didn't mind interrupting his sermon. In fact, he seemed to require it.

"Amen!" March's little voice joined the choir of voices.

"Amen!" Amanda whispered. *Magnificent.* She turned, and the entire crowd was on their feet, praising God with their clapping. Mrs. Milford was there as well, in the last row, smiling and nodding her head. She wasn't standing up, but she clearly approved of the goings-on.

Virgil took the Bible and sat down in a chair at the front, whipped out his hanky, and wiped his face.

What a wonderful speaker. He could do a lot to advocate for the new little town. But where? The state house? All the way to Washington City? How could she help him to that endeavor?

She didn't know how, but she would. Virgil had a powerful work to do, and she aimed to help him.

Only one thing nibbled at the edge of her consciousness. Why had Virgil not opened the Bible at all to read the original scripture? He'd given the location of the story, but, still, the minister always read the Scripture.

The children of the fiery furnace was a wonderful parable of faith—and so vivid. The thought of the heat touching the body, always something to think about. Coming from Virgil, a man used to dealing with fire, made it somehow all the more real.

But what was the idol he spoke about so repeatedly? Idols in their world? The former slaves were just trying to do right by farming the land and paying Mrs. Milford her due.

The newest thing in the hamlet was her. She was the shiny new thing in the hamlet.

A hot blush, as if she had been the one placed into the fiery furnace, spread all over her. March looked up at her. "You all right, Mamma?"

Amanda embraced her. "I'm fine, child."

But she wasn't. Was Virgil's sermon a way of telling the people to stay true to themselves, despite what learning had to tell them?

She made her eyes meet Virgil's as everyone stood to sing a spiritual song about Meshach, Shadrach, and Abednego. He sang in a deep bass, his voice reaching into her and making the warm places even warmer.

It hit her, all of a sudden, why he should hate her and not want her there. No, it wasn't because she was the shiny new thing. It was because of him.

He couldn't read.

Her fingertips tingled as she raised her voice in a song she did not know and rubbed her hands together.

He didn't want people to know he was illiterate.

His shame at his illiteracy transferred to her and washed through her, turning to joy as her fingertips tingled. This would be how she made her marriage. God had brought her here for a reason. Now she understood. She would be of use like she'd promised to him under that tree. In thinking about the promise, she was taking her wedding vow all over again—another day later.

Guess they might have had some spiritual songs up there in Ohio. His new wife joined the song as if she knew what she were singing. Dressed in her blue and white striped wedding dress, he was struck anew by her prettiness and her dewy, pecan-brown complexion. Amanda was a wonder and a blessing all at the same time.

God, help me to know what to do with your blessings and not waste them. Got to know how to enjoy the blessing.

Lord, he was going to have to court his own wife.

Judging from her reaction yesterday, she would not be opposed to it. Until she found out all about him.

The spiritual came to an end, and he added an additional prayer. *Let Amanda come to know me for me and not feel resentment or hate when she knows how I don't deserve to be a mayor or anything else.*

When the service ended, she stepped up to him and clutched at his sleeve. "Virgil, that was amazing. I've never seen anything like what you did. It was beautiful."

Instead of feeling flattered, his heart sank. How would he possibly be able to avoid disappointing her anymore? She deserved better than him, someone who could read as she did. Mandy had all that education, and when she found out, she wouldn't want to be stuck with him anymore.

He should have told her before the wedding. Might have saved a lot of grief and hurt. When she went north to inquire about additional teachers, she might even meet an old beau and forget all about him.

The possibility created an ache in his heart which spread across his chest. It hurt too much to even think about, and he patted her hand on his arm, saying nothing to her. But saying everything at the same time.

CHAPTER NINE

After church, parishioners gathered on a knoll behind the schoolhouse for a fish fry and picnic to celebrate their preacher's marriage. Amanda and Virgil hardly interacted in the entire melee following church. It was touching, though, how people were genuinely happy for them, and she could tell that many felt uplifted by the deep truths of Virgil's wonderful sermon.

Which still sent chills down her spine. What a wonderful speaker. She had heard Frederick Douglass speak in Oberlin. Virgil equaled the fiery spirit of his oratory in every way. How to help him be more beyond Milford was the puzzle. Mrs. Milford might be a help in part of that.

But there was still morning to come and the first day of school. Despite getting up early to fix breakfast for her family, when they arrived at the little schoolhouse there were people waiting on them.

"School will start as I ring the bell."

"Didn't know, miss. We sorry," a tall, older girl said.

"Fine. What are your names, children?"

The girl gestured to herself, then to the shoeless boy next to her "I'm Lena, and this here is my brother Mac. We walked plenty far to get here. Sorry we miss the church, but we don't have a mule."

"Where are you from?" Amanda unlocked the door and let the children inside. March danced in ahead of her, but the new children came cautiously behind.

"Crumpton. Next town over. Missionary place started a school there in the winter, and it got burned down."

A chill went through her. "Didn't the missionary say they would replace the school?"

"They did, ma'am, but that was back in January. I sure enjoyed the school. So they still building, trying to get a teacher, but we going to come here. For now."

"It's still dark outside. You came all that way in the dark?"

Lena straightened. "I got shoes. Mac doesn't, but he make it okay."

"I like school." Mac's eyes, shining with expectation, burned at her soul.

Her father would have known how to handle this situation. Her heart ripped in two. She missed him so very much. His kind questioning, his authoritative posture, and his intelligence all would have combined to make him so useful here.

I can't do this alone, God. I need help. I am so lost.

At that moment, Virgil stomped through the door.

"Came to see who you was talking to here."

Amanda made the necessary introductions. "These pupils have come from very far to continue their schooling. A very admirable thing."

"Our school got burned."

"Yes. Heard about that."

"The Missionary Society said they would rebuild, but they haven't. Teachers are apparently hard to come by around here."

Virgil coughed. "Guess so."

"Have you had breakfast?" Amanda asked the children.

"Mamma gave us some bread to bring us here, but it was awhile ago."

"Here." She opened her lunch pail and pulled out her ham sandwich. "It's not breakfast food, but it will do."

Mac's eyes grew. "Sure will."

Amanda divided the sandwich as neatly as she could and gave half to each child. The children chomped at the sandwiches.

Her husband's eyes saddened as he watched the children. Finally he turned to her. "If you okay, I'm going to the smithy."

"Thank you for checking."

"I'm the mayor. I'm supposed to."

Well, of course. It's not because he cared for her or anything like that. That would not be allowed. Would it? The thought that he might care for her made her body fall chill on the hot day.

After he exited, a flood of children of all ages came inside and occupied every bench. Even when she crowded them onto the benches, the older ones still stood in the back and eventually slid down the walls to sit on the floor and take in the morning's alphabet lesson.

Certainly, the two children from the burned-down school would think this all repetitive and strange. But they seemed as captivated as the rest of the children, so she continued her teaching.

The morning went swiftly on. They went outside to eat lunch, and there was a festive air as if a picnic were going on. Their fun gladdened her heart—the children were so happy to have the opportunity to learn. She watched from the front porch of the school as they drank water from the pump and played games.

A carriage with one horse came trotting up the long roadway. She shaded her eyes to see who it was. Mrs. Milford.

Amanda cleared her throat. Being friends with the plantation mistress would go a long way to helping Virgil. She waited while Mrs. Milford pulled up to the front of the schoolhouse, then stepped off the porch to greet her. She made a circle around the schoolhouse in her carriage and pulled up to the schoolhouse door, keeping hold of the reins in her hands.

The woman leaned out to greet her. "Amanda. How is everything going?"

"Well, ma'am. Thank you. Learning letters today."

"The Mission needed to send slates for the children, but they didn't do it. I'm inclined to bring them myself."

"If you could, it would be a big help. Thank you for your kindness."

This was what Mrs. Milford lived for, to be petted and thanked. What an existence, waiting for other people to realize their gratitude and say nice things. So sad.

"I want to help in any way."

"Ma'am, you said you taught your own children. Would you consider helping now?"

"Me?" Mrs. Milford stood still and let her skirts blow all around her. Amanda's skirts, cut down to size, kept appropriately still. "Do you mean to say you can't do your job?"

"No, ma'am. I'm saying that I need help. There's so many of them."

"Well, I'm sure that you will figure it out. You're a very bright girl, and I went to great expense to bring you here. And you went to great trouble to stay, marrying Virgil and all."

Mrs. Milford smiled, and Amanda quaked inside. What did she mean by that? Had the woman expected her to say no?

Mrs. Milford flicked a fly away from her. "Virgil's a very good man. He can go places with the right woman beside him."

"I sense that. I'll do anything to help him."

"I saw that about you when you came. That you would be willing to do anything to help your people—even marry a man you barely knew."

Be still and know that I am God.

Was Mrs. Milford playing some kind of game with her? She considered how cautious Virgil was in his dealings with her. Why? Amanda stilled her small skirt before she spoke. "It's certainly difficult in this world when a woman has no protection, no family to call her own. When my father died, I came to understand that I would have to strike out in the world and make my own family. It certainly seems that I've been able to do that here in Milford. And for that I praise God."

"I see what you say. The war killed off my two sons. My daughter-in-law who has the girls has taken them somewhere. I don't even know where. I have no one but the Negroes here. That's why I've wanted to help them find a path in life." Tears slid down Mrs. Milford's withered face.

"It's the Christian thing to do."

"It certainly is. I could do nothing else."

"I'm pleased to hear it. I'll call the children back in now. If you wish to join us anytime, please do."

She stepped away from Mrs. Milford, clutching her striped skirt. The war had taken so much from so many that Amanda felt for the woman's sorrow. Still, she didn't want Mrs. Milford's slant on life impacting the work she had to do with these children. Or Virgil.

Standing on the rise of the hill and looking down into the town, she waved in the direction of the smithy. It didn't matter if he could see her or not; she just wanted him to know she was there for him.

Virgil ate the biscuit sandwich Amanda had packed for him and imagined he could see the schoolhouse on the crest of the hill. He imagined her waving to him in greeting. The thought warmed him. For once in his life, he had done something to be helpful to a woman.

A good and worthy thing.

Washing his hands and face at the pump, the clip clop of Mrs. Milford's high-stepping horse sounded across the hard red dirt. There was a long afternoon of work ahead, but he should check in with her to make sure everything was all right. "How do, ma'am?"

"Everything all right, Virgil?"

"Just fine, ma'am."

"I just came from seeing the school. Lots of folk from miles around wanting to come to be educated. A wonderful thing. Never did agree with that practice in the old days."

"No, ma'am."

"But it didn't help you, did it?"

"Everything get to be too late for me by the time I buy myself away." He patted her horse, pulling a carrot from his work apron pocket and giving it to him. "Nothing to be done."

Mrs. Milford shook her head. "I don't know. All those children in there, they're all learning at once. Maybe adults want to learn how to read and write as well."

"Maybe. It be harder for some than others."

"Had a visitor recently. He said they were floating ideas for candidates for the state senate maybe in the next couple of years."

"They sure don't want you to run, do they, ma'am?"

Mrs. Milford held her chest as she laughed. "Goodness, no. What could a woman do? No, he was asking if I knew anyone who would be interested in such a proposition."

"And?"

"Virgil, you can be so trying sometimes. Of course I suggested you."

"Suggested me? Without asking?"

"Well, I was going to tell you."

Just like the old days. "Nice of you."

"Don't be smart. I had to make sure you were the right one. Now you have a wife and a very successful school going here. There's so much you could be showing them in the capital. How a Negro can do things."

The idea was certainly tempting. "Now you married me off and want me to leave my wife. Why?"

Mrs. Milford regarded him. "I see that matters much to you."

"I'm a man of my word. If I promise to take care of someone, then that's what I want to do."

"And why you are so suitable for more than being a mayor. Speaking of, there's some papers you need to file in Milledgeville. You'll have to be away for a day or two."

"Wife need to know if I'm leaving. Then we let you know."

"Think about it."

Virgil fixed Mrs. Milford with his own regarding look. "You think Negroes will vote?"

"Someday. Not all of the whites will, or can now. A lot of them respect you. I think you have more than a fair chance."

"Maybe then. I'll talk with my wife."

A strange smile played about her lips. "Yes. Please do speak about it with her. She must be a part of all decisions about your future from now on. We'll talk soon."

Mrs. Milford slapped the reins on her horse and went on. Why was she being so mysterious? Who knew what she was thinking? Or what any woman thought?

Not my trouble.

He went inside the smithy and worked at his anvil, just as he knew he should.

But he didn't stay there long.

What was going on at the top of that hill? Now Mrs. Milford wanted to draw him into something even bigger. How could he do that, given what he was? Who he was?

"Calling it a day, Isaac. Close up for me."

Isaac stopped beating on a shoe. "You leaving?"

No, he never left early, but he was married now. Things changed for him.

He rode on his favorite mare, Pie, up the hill to the school-house where the door was wide open, the building fairly bursting with children. Some of the parents sat on the porch.

Virgil tied Pie up. "What's going on here?"

"Shh. She got the door open. Just wondering what's going on in there, sir. Hope you don't mind."

"That's for her to say. This is her schoolhouse."

"Wish she teach the parents something," Calla Baxter pushed back the scarf on her head.

He did too. "Have you asked her?"

"Naw, but since we in the fields all day, working lots elsewhere at night, she might not agree."

"Lord, I would love to read the Good Book for myself. Wouldn't that be something?" Calla fretted out loud.

Sure would. He paused on the front steps and listened to Amanda's patient explanations about the sounds the letters made.

Every student said it right along with her. He did too, moving his lips.

They were all captivated by her. Maybe he was too, although she would be the last person he would tell. He had never met anyone like Amanda Stewart before, ever. Well, Amanda Smithson. The name he'd made for himself was her name now, and he wanted to get on his knees and praise the Almighty for his mercies.

In minutes, the shuffle of feet started a stampede, and a large throng of children, shoed and shoeless, made their way to the door. Virgil got up to make way for the children. He surely didn't want to get run over.

March danced through the classroom, her thin body moving to some invisible beat she herself only knew. How had she behaved in school today? If she had given her mamma the least hard time, he would let her know about it.

Several children followed Amanda's skirts as she strode forward to the door. Emerging onto the front porch, she raised her eyebrows in surprise at the multitude that waited for her. She smiled at everyone else, but her eyes were only for him. He liked it.

Calla spoke. "Mrs. Teacher," she said to Amanda. "Wondering if you let the parents come learn too? I want to read the Good Book to myself."

Amanda turned to Calla and he had to stop himself from breathing out his disappointment.

"What a wonderful notion. It's a comfort to read the Bible, but it's harder reading than other things. Might take some time."

Another woman, one he didn't know spoke up. "I wouldn't mind. I could learn right along with my children here. They come to your school today."

The woman's face radiated a light Virgil understood. Virgil turned to Amanda to see if she could see the woman's hope. She looked tired. He was about to say something, but she stayed his arm. The feel of her dainty hand on him was calming and reassuring.

"I don't know what I could do to help the grown-ups. Maybe Saturday school? After the half day of work? It wouldn't be good to do it after church on Sunday. That's God's time, and I wouldn't want to impose on that."

"No, indeed," he added.

The woman rubbed her hands together. "Please think on it. Saturday would be better than nothing."

"I have to get home and prepare dinner for my family," Amanda said in the gentlest of ways, "but there is no need for you to come so far. I can send word by the children if you like."

"Oh yes, ma'am. And thank you for considering it."

They watched the little family walk down the road, braced for the long, long walk back to Crumpton.

"They'll need a school too," he said.

"They will, but I'll do as I must. I'm glad I stayed here, Mr. Smithson, even though you tried to send me away."

Her gentle tone hit him harder than he liked. He cleared his throat. "Well now, that's not exactly true. I didn't want you to stay here under those circumstances, living by yourself without protection. Especially not with some in the town who might not like all these schools being built up for Negro children." He sobered. "Teaching adults would be a different thing, maybe even more risky."

Mandy paused, and her lovely silken brows drew together on her heart-shaped face. "I gathered that. Which is why I didn't say yes right away. I wouldn't mind doing a Saturday school, or even something in the evenings, but it might not be viewed well. What do you think Mrs. Milford might say?"

"We ask tomorrow. She was by today."

"I know. She came to see the school. I get the sense that she's lonely, so I invited her to help. With forty children and maybe adults, I need the help. But she's confined to her ideals of what she should be doing. Oh, well. Maybe she'll be like me free herself of all of that someday to do a real work."

"She say I have to go to Milledgeville, the state capital, to file some papers as mayor."

She put her hand on his arm. "Oh, good. While you're there, you might make inquiries about Crumpton getting a schoolhouse. You can also post correspondence to Oberlin about a teacher."

Virgil frowned. "While I'm away, you be unprotected up here."

"You can build more houses on this rise, and other families will move in. Maybe I'll get a gun."

"You, a tiny?" He laughed at the thought.

"If it's for my protection, I might need one."

Might not be a bad idea.

"I'll tell you what. An even exchange. You teach me to shoot a gun."

"Okay. For what?"

"I'll teach you how to read and write."

He stepped from her, feeling the blood circulating in his body, something he'd never thought of before.

She had figured him out. There it was. The very thing he feared.

He stepped off the schoolhouse's porch and unlaced Pie from the stand.

"Virgil!"

He led the horse to the barn, his unworthiness slipping from him like a stench. He needed to be as far away from Mandy as possible.

No need to taint her with it.

CHAPTER TEN

Why didn't he answer when she called him? What had she done wrong? Had she offended him?

Virgil had so much potential, so much going for him, that she honestly believed it was God's design to help him here. Still, that night he choked down the dinner she'd made and did not speak to her. Was this a sensitive issue with him? That the adults needed to learn, including himself and she was already overwhelmed?

The next morning, more of the parents sat on the front porch of the school and listened before they had to go into the fields. Should she have a Saturday school? Maybe there Virgil would be comfortable.

She sought his council that night in hopes that he respond to her, rather than grunt.

"I'm still thinking about the Saturday school or maybe the day should be extended a bit so parents can come into the schoolroom and learn with the children at the end of the day. Do you think the parents and children share lessons at night?"

"How am I supposed to know what folks do at home?"

"They're your friends and knowledgeable acquaintances, Virgil."

"I don't get into other folks business when it ain't mine. Unlike some people from up north who want to come south and see about business that ain't none of their concern."

"How can you say that? You sent for me. You put out a call for the schoolteacher."

"We put out a call for a schoolmaster. You come. That was the difference."

Well, there was no response for that.

She wiped her hands on her apron and walked outside. Clearly, Virgil didn't want her around, didn't like her. She was naught more than a hired girl.

How would she find a way? Any way or place here?

She bent down to sit on the grass. Strange. She'd thought she would be able to charm him, just as she had other men in Ohio, even Charles Henry.

She shuddered. Conjuring him up in her mind didn't help. She clenched the grass, feeling the green leach into her palms.

Charles Henry had her living. She was certain of it. He was the reason she had to come down here and be subjected to marriage to a man who didn't want her so she would be "protected."

All during the war she had this understanding, just as Mr. Lincoln did, of this entity called the Union and that the South consisted of mean and unruly people who wanted to break away from that Union to keep people enslaved. The war was over and slavery gone, but had she become enslaved herself? The fine education her father had provided her was no protection. That was clear enough.

The features of her father reformed themselves into her mind, and hot tears slid down her cheeks. She wiped them away, so ashamed that they were the first tears she'd bothered to shed for him, but thinking of him and Virgil's thorough rejection of her made her feel so lonely and lost.

"You need to come in. Night coming down."

Virgil's deep voice stirred her again, and she quashed the feeling down one more time. *Why does he do that to me?*

It was silly to be angry at him as if he were doing wrong, but was it wrong to be stirred by him?

Once again, the higher tenor timbre of her father's voice came to her. "When you find the right husband, his voice will be as a call unto you and will stir you like the wind, Amanda. That's when you know."

Hot tears slid faster because that was how she felt just now. But this man didn't feel like that about her.

"What do you care? If I were gone, you could send for your precious schoolmaster. I would be out of the way." She smoothed the braids in the knot at the back of her neck and defied him to say something different.

He didn't. He just looked at her in the same way he always did, as if she were some strange animal he didn't know quite how to interact with.

"Building is full of people. They need a teacher. That's you."

She dared to prod him, just a bit. "And you don't need me?"

His strange look disappeared, and a sad one took its place.

Maybe he'd be willing to speak, now that March wasn't here. It hit her like a lightning bolt—his position in the community, his position as a father had to be protected.

"There was no call to speak to me like that, Virgil."

"I know. I apologized."

Now she was a little speechless. She didn't expect the apology to come so fast. "You don't want to learn."

"Didn't say that."

"What is it then?"

Now she was in the position of student, learning how to respond to this man without wounding his pride. She let the silence stay, her heart pounding and her hands clenched the grass again.

He sat down beside her. Not right next to her, but in the same vicinity so it was clear that they were not enemies at least. "I can't."

"Can't what?"

"Learn how to read. I tried. I make letters; they come out looking strange. Even Mrs. Milford can't help."

"She couldn't."

"No."

"Who wrote up the letter?"

"Mrs. Milford. She signed my name."

Amanda nodded. "I don't believe you can't be taught."

"I try to learn while I was away from Milford. Even Mrs. Milford try. Three, four times. But what do you know? You just a tiny."

"I may be a tiny, but I'm mighty in God's eyes. I believe everyone can be taught."

"Well, that's just foolishness. I take on apprentices at the forge. Some can't learn. I just let them go."

"I don't know much about what you do as a blacksmith, but it's not the same in reading and writing."

Quiet stayed them. Did he believe her? She felt as if she were fishing and had to stay still and make subtle noises to reel him in.

"I knew when I saw you, you find me out. That's why I didn't want you to stay. Women can be kind of sneaky, using their minds to figure things out."

"Well, thank you." *I think.*

"I shouldn't be the mayor."

"What does that have to do with anything?"

"Should be someone who can read and write."

"But you're the one who's had a lot of experience seeing the world. That's important."

"Maybe."

"You have good judgment. People trust you. And you speak wonderfully. You know about Frederick Douglass?"

He nodded.

"You speak as well as he does. You have a good understanding of the Bible and God's words. That makes people see His light."

Virgil gripped the grass himself, but did not pull at the blades. He'd probably sewn grass seed into this ground. She stopped her grabbing and pulling. The land had a different appeal when you saw it from the viewpoint of those who tilled it.

"Can't read the Bible myself. Everything I know, I 'membered."

"That means you have an excellent memory. I've read the Good Book many times myself and you say what's in there. Virgil, you have a mind."

"And I can't get to my mind to focus."

"If I tell you that it may take a little more time and a little more work, will you let me teach you a little bit at night?"

"We needs to get our sleep. I got long days at the forge. And now, if I do this thing up in the state house, that's more." He fixed her with a sharp gaze. "Maybe you got some learning to do yourself. How to take care of animals while I'm gone. This here house. That kind of thing."

A light dawned. "That's more we'll exchange. You teach me to take care of the animals. I will teach you how to read and write."

"After March goes to bed."

"Yes. In that little space of time after she goes to bed. That will be fine."

"And I teach you about the animals in the morning. A deal." He extended his hand to her.

She shouldn't shake the hand of a strange man. Except this man was her husband. So it was fine to shake hands with him.

She put her hand inside of his, and his hand swallowed hers up whole, his touch and hold so, so gentle.

A melty feeling stirred inside of her, and a thrill went into the tips of her high top shoes. She cleared her throat to ensure that she sounded in full control of herself. "It's a deal, Mr. Smithson. I mean, Virgil. We begin your lessons tonight."

With a sharp quick tug, she pulled her hand free so she would remain in control. She must always be in control.

You're just dumb.
You'll never learn to read.
You belong in the fields with the rest of the dumb animals.

He'd heard it all. All those years after he'd bought his freedom from the Milfords and had been forced to leave Sally's side with baby March in her arms. He'd wandered all over the north part of the country, being free, earning a living with his anvil here and there.

Being up north was supposed to mean better. It was supposed to mean people believed he was a man and that he could do man things. Like write.

Those slate pencils were so small. The pencil always slipped from his hands. His hard calluses made the slate pencil hard to hold. He would press too hard, and the letters would look wrong.

Now he would have to look like some dumb man in front of this Amanda Stewart who had come into his life and changed everything.

Saturday was tomorrow, and some of the parents would come to a weekend school session. She would probably want to go to bed early.

So he did the chores extra long, so he wouldn't have to go inside. He could make a bed of hay in the barn, with the horses and his milk cow, just to avoid her. But he was efficient about his work, and the time came when he was done. He couldn't avoid going into his own house anymore.

A man shouldn't be afraid to go in his own house.

He had worked too hard for this house, after years of wandering. He had built it with the money he'd saved to buy Sally and March from the Milfords. Only he was weeks too late. After the slaves were freed, he made his way back to Georgia, but Sally was already gone. Then he left to find her and she died in his arms.

So he built a house. For March. Because that's what Sally would have wanted.

But the slick wetness on his palms and the stirrings in his stomach long after dinner was over made it hard to think about anything except Amanda. "Just a tiny."

What a tiny she was. That beautiful heart-shaped face. Her dimpled cheeks. Her small, soft hands and steady voice when she spoke to her students. The way she spoke to March and looked at her, her kind eyes full of love and hope, not with an expectation that she was meant to serve.

Soon those eyes would turn to him in disappointment, and he didn't know if he could take that.

He didn't have to do this. He would just go upstairs to his room and get ready for bed. He had a long day of work tomorrow too. Saturday was no day off. He didn't stay down at the forge the whole day, but he would still see about the business of people, make sure marriages were doing okay, settle any disputes. Maybe even report in to Mrs. Milford. But he did not have to subject himself to—

"Virgil?" Her calm voice called him, but his insides didn't respond with calm. They quaked like a newborn calf's legs.

"I'm going on up." He put strength into his voice. He knew he could sound intimidating when he wished, so he wished.

"I thought we were going to work together. I put March in bed some time ago." A note of disappointment echoed in her words.

Lord, tell me what to do. He would make her mad either way. "Tired. Got to get rest." He swallowed hard.

"Me too. So this won't take long."

Won't take long? She didn't know what she was about to deal with. Before he knew it, she came around the corner from the kitchen and stood in front of him with the lamp from the dining table. "We don't want to waste this last little bit of light. Come on."

She took him by the hand and guided him into the near-darkened room, but when she put the lamp on the center of the table, the light filled the room. She guided him to a chair, and he sat.

"There's a slate for you here. I've started with five letters. I'll show you how to shape them, and we'll say them together."

With increasing dread clenching his stomach, he looked around for that little slip of a slate pencil. Maybe when it slipped through his clumsy fingers, it would get lost on the floor and be too hard to find.

But on the table in front of him he saw the longest slate pencil he had ever seen.

"Where that come from?"

"What, Virgil?" She sat across from him, hands folded, the picture of calm.

"To write on the slate with. The pencil."

"I made it."

"You made it?"

Her long eyelashes blinked. "There's a difference between the way you teach adults and the way you teach children. My father taught me that. Differences in the examples used and in the tools used." She lowered her head, and the shininess of her hair glistened in the lamplight. "You have large hands. There's no way you could hold a regular slate pencil. So I created one. Just for you."

Who was this woman? How could he even begin to do what she wanted so he didn't fall short of what she expected? "Oh. I see."

"Pick it up, and form the first letter. There. *A.*"

He picked up the pencil, and she came to him. Her deft fingers worked over his large hand, forming them to fit the pencil, just as if he were just another student, but the jolts of feeling that shot from her fingers shocked him.

When she was done, a larger part of the pencil extended out with a knobby part in the middle where the two parts had been joined together. The pencil felt good and secure in his hand. "How did you make it?"

Her black eyes danced with amusement. "My goodness, Virgil. You're a blacksmith and a mayor. God willing, maybe more, and you mean I bested you? A tiny like me?"

He cleared his throat, relishing the comfortable feel of the cool pencil between his fingers. Maybe he could do this. "I don't know about all of that now."

"I believe it," she proclaimed.

Her eyes blinked but never left his face. How tempting to look away from her cool steady gaze, he just couldn't. If he knew how to blush in embarrassment, he might have done it, but that just wasn't in him.

"That so?" Probably best to keep steady in some way.

"I spoke it. I've prayed about it. And it's here. It's up to you to take the steps." She gestured to the slate, her pretty braids shaking back and forth. " *A.*"

"*A.*"

"A circle around and a tail off the back."

The pencil betrayed him and shifted forward to the tips of his fingers, nearly slipping away. A burning sensation rose from his stomach as he tried to press the pencil in the direction he wanted it to go. And it wouldn't.

Please, God.

Before he knew or understood what had happened, she was beside him, her hand on his, putting the pencil back into the right place and making the letter on the slate.

It looked good too.

"Again," she said in a firm teacher voice.

He wouldn't be the one to disobey her. "Yes."

"Speak it with me. Circle around, a tail in the back."

"Circle around, tail in back."

He tried not to thrill to the way her hand felt on his, but he couldn't help it. The room, a room he'd built with his own hands, began to close in on him.

"Another time."

"Circle around, tail in back."

"Say it exactly. A circle around, a tail in the back."

Well, then. "A circle around, a tail in the back."

She let his hand go. "Try now."

Beads of sweat popped onto his forehead. *Please, God.* "Circle around, a tail in the back."

He removed his hand to look at the letter. It was smaller than the ones they'd made together. But it was there.

"Open it up more the next time. Try it again and say it again."

"A circle around, a tail in the back." He lifted his hand again and noticed, with relief, that it looked better. He had done it.

"Better. See? Now think the way you make the letter and say the sound."

She stepped away and sat across from him. He didn't know whether to look at her or the slate.

He chose to look at her.

Her mouth was slightly opened, and her small pink tongue formed the sound. He was supposed to do it too, but it was more fun watching her do it.

"Virgil. Cat."

"Oh. Caaaat."

"Shape the letter as you say it. Think of the shape."

With great reluctance, he took his eyes off of her and looked down at the slate. A circle around, a tail in the back. "Caaaat."

"You don't have to press so hard. Try again."

"Caaaat." He moved his hand away, almost too afraid to look.

"Wonderful!" She clasped her hands together.

"It is?" He looked down at the second letter. It looked pretty fine to him. He had done it himself.

"It is." She sat back in the chair, then stood up and gathered a book from the table. "I'll trust you to turn down the wick. Goodnight, Virgil."

"That's it?" He laid the pencil across the slate.

"I told you it wouldn't take much of your time."

Disappointment washed over him like a dip in the creek. "I—I thought I was going to learn more letters."

She fixed him with a stare. "You decide what you want to do, Virgil. You master this one, and I'll show you more tomorrow. If that's what you want. Good night."

She slipped up the stairs, quiet as anything.

He sat back in his seat. Well. His first lesson. With Mandy. And it hadn't gone as badly as he'd feared.

There was still a bit of the oil left in the lamp, so he picked up the pencil, fitted it into his hand, and made those *a*'s over and over again, thinking about the sun in her smile when he managed to do it right, covering the slate front and back so that in the morning she could see how he had tried.

Just for her.

Chapter Eleven

When Amanda came downstairs for breakfast the next day, she picked up the slate. Pleasure rushed through her at the sight of the slate with *a's* on the front side and *a's* on the back, some smeared. Amazing.

She could trace the progression from the *a's* where Virgil had been less confident to the ones he had done perfectly.

She knew he would be that kind of student. Yet she prayed to find a way to reach him, to show him his own possibility. Living here for such a short time had shown her that these former slaves had just emerged from a war of their own. Now it was a battle to get them to understand how important they were—for themselves. They were valuable people—it was the chief reason for the war. Still, when people learned a different way, it was hard to get them to see the truth of their lives.

What of Virgil? He differed since he had his freedom before the war. What had he learned in all of those years of wandering? Lessons of life, both positive and negative, to be sure. She'd need to convince him that those years of freedom, coupled with his skills and powerful oratory, made him a possible leader of the people. She would be there as his teacher to help him see his worth.

Or as his wife.

Hot, red embarrassment came into her fingertips, and she set the slate down. Yes, in that way as well. Sometimes she forgot she was Amanda Smithson now, since they had no other relationship beyond the church and the school. No relationship for them, but just last night…Had he felt it too? The connection between them? She touched the edge of the slate with her fingertips, remembering the feel of his smooth palm beneath her own.

"Did I do right?"

She jumped. "Oh. Good morning, Virgil. You startled me."

"I'm sorry, Mandy. Just wanted to know if you liked the look of the letters."

"This is fine. You understood what I meant. Practice. A fine start indeed."

"Good. We can do some more later."

"If you like." She nodded her head in his direction. "Or you can come to my afternoon school today."

A scowl almost crossed his face. Then it cleared. "I might do that."

"Good. I'm going into town this morning. Should I take March with me or leave her here with you?"

"What do you mean?"

"I have some necessities to pick up. I wanted to borrow the wagon to drive into Crumpton."

"Woman, are you crazy? You can't just go into Crumpton in the wagon by yourself."

"Why not? That was how Mrs. Milford brought back the slates."

He gave a half laugh, stirring something inside of her. He wasn't laughing at her, was he?

"You're not Mrs. Milford. That's the difference. Town has a different meaning for a tiny like you. Especially a pretty tiny with brown skin, and you new?" Virgil shook his head. "I ain't doing nothing that important today. I'll take you in."

"I know how to drive a wagon."

"I know. You knows how to do a lot of things, but you haven't lived in the South long enough to *know.* Trust me in this."

Now she shook her head. The Georgia pines looked so peaceful as they swayed in the breeze. How could there be harm in them?

One of the hallmarks of a good teacher was to know what you knew and what you didn't. She didn't know these Georgia woods. "Fine. I just didn't know if you had duties in the town or at the forge."

"I said, nothing that important. Go on ahead and get breakfast together. I'll let Isaac know where I'ma be this morning."

"I believe he's coming to the afternoon class."

There was a grunt from him again. "Going to take care of the livestock. I'll be back."

In the kitchen she fixed some bacon and a small pan of biscuits from the flour they had left. She had not anticipated her desire to go to town would stir up this kind of upset in him, but, then again, they knew so little about one another. She would just have to get used to different reactions from him. He was so mercurial. How would she ever get to the place where she pleased him instead of troubling him?

Dear God, help me to help Virgil understand what I need from him. I don't want to be a trouble to him. I want to be a help in whatever way I can.

One thing she could do for him would be to give him nourishment for his body. Then maybe he would understand that she could nourish his spirit as well.

Town? This woman acted as if she could just swing into town, go where she pleased, and that was it. He had learned, many times the hard way, that whenever you went to a new town, the best way to play it was low and slow.

Eyes low to the ground with a slow approach. That always worked best. They wouldn't mind taking your money or whatever good things you to trade, but it was all about how to approach folk.

He looked at her, perched up on the edge of the wagon seat like a bright bird.

Behind him, in the open wagon, March scrambled around like a puppy, as if she had no better sense. Well, he had only been back one year, so she was more under Pauline's teachings, but she should know better.

"Be still, March."

He used his stern tone, so she would listen to him, but she fidgeted. No wonder the child could hardly keep any meat on her bones. She stayed in movement constantly.

Even her moving worried him. Folks saw you moving around like that, and they assume you a good, quick worker and give you more work to do, just like an old mule. He didn't want March broken down like that.

Bad times is over.

He blinked again as he traversed the road. Sometimes, it was hard to remember. Freedom had been with him for six years, but it was new to March who had just reached the age when they would start working her. He didn't have to worry about her appearing to be a good worker.

Still, Mrs. Milford's offers to show her how to sew and such made him unhappy. He didn't like it. Best he be the one to deal with Mrs. Milford. He had seen enough to know how to deal with her.

"Beautiful day." His wife spoke out of nowhere.

"Be too hot for too long. We need to get what we need in town and get home."

She perked up. "Yes, for the afternoon school session."

He slapped the reins on the horses which made them go just a bit faster. "Yeah, I know."

"Good. I can expect to see you there."

"May have town business. We'll see."

"We should send around a general notice that if anyone has town business in Milford from now on, they can come to the schoolhouse in the mornings where you can weigh in on disputes, marry people, bless babies, that kind of thing. After that, folks can stay for the Saturday school."

This woman here, she was just too smart for her own good. Of course it was a good idea. Still what made her believe that it would work so well in Milford?

"We'll see."

"Virgil, you are the officiate in the community. You simply cannot exhaust yourself, going to see people in their homes. Papa used to ride circuit as a lawyer, and it just wore him out. And I missed him so when he was gone."

She inclined her pretty bonneted head to March. Mandy wore a soft bonnet today, a bit more old-fashioned, but still appropriate to her new status as a married lady. He liked the way the lace framed her face. Like a picture. "You don't want March longing for her papa, would you now?"

"She see me enough."

"Papa, you was gone a long time afore. I remembers when you came back. Pauline had to tell me you was my papa. I didn't know who you were."

The sad little tone in her voice made his hands sweat. He gripped the reins—which wasn't good 'cause there was salt in that sweat which ate up a good set of reins. He gathered them in one hand and waved first one hand, then another, in the air.

"Why were you gone so long, Virgil?"

He turned to regard her, and it struck him that there was no judgment in her tone. She honestly wanted to know.

"Old times meant, when I bought myself from the Milfords, I had to leave home. Couldn't stay here in Georgia. It was against the law."

"My." Mandy put a hand to her heart. "What an awful conundrum."

What she mean to say?

"A problem. You had your wife and daughter here, and you were forced to leave them."

Up over the rise, the small pine forest town of Crumpton rose before them, and he felt a slight kink in his stomach work itself out. "It was old times. Just best not to talk on it."

"It had to impact you."

She laid her light touch on his arm, like a butterfly, and her eyes stared deep into his. For just that moment in time, he believed there was someone on the earth who felt as he felt about things, someone he could talk to.

He shook it off. *Fool talk.* "Maybe, but if I thought about it all the time, I wouldn't be able to do what I have to do for my family. Including you."

"Well, of course." She drew her hand back, and sadness came into his heart. Just for a second. He had to be firm to show her how to be in the South.

"Since you my family"—He pulled the horses to a stop before they could enter the Crumpton environs—"you do what I say. Keep your eyes down to the ground. Go in slow. Say yes, sir. No, sir. Yes, ma'am. No, ma'am." Although he doubted they would run into any women. Women on Saturdays were at home, getting ready for church.

"Fine, Virgil."

"Let me see you do it." He swiveled to face March, and her bright black-button eyes shifted away from him to the side of the wagon. "That fine, March. Now you."

"Me? Whatever for?"

"Because I say you got to. Do it."

He had never before noticed the light brown glints in her eyes, but he did now because they disappeared. Had he solved a puzzle? Those glints were what made her eyes so merry and happy when she looked out on the world. Now, because of what he said and where they were, they disappeared. She dropped her gaze and tilted her head toward the floorboard of the wagon. "Good. Keep it that way, and we just might make it through this day."

Taking up the reins again, Virgil guided the horses into town and tied them up at the general store. He helped Mandy down from the seat, offered his arm, and escorted her into the store.

Surprisingly, there were no customers inside. The town, built out of white pine, wasn't nothing more special than Milford. They just had things Milford didn't—a store and a paper and turpentine mill. No smithy, though. That was what he had to offer.

He stood near the front door, Mandy on his arm, and waited. He put a hand on March's shoulder. *Please, be still. Don't move, daughter.* Because he prayed it, he guessed, she was still. For once. *Amen.*

The white-mustached man behind the counter beckoned them forward.

"Virgil. What you doing here so early this morning? Who is this?"

"Mr. Daley. This my wife. Amanda Smithson."

"I heard you'd gotten married, Virgil. This is some surprise. Hadn't heard you were sparking anyone over to Milford. She around from somewhere else?"

Mandy lifted her head.

Spoke.

Directly to Mr. Daley.

"I'm from Ohio, sir."

Dear God, please let us get home safe today.

Mr. Daily's mustache twitched, just a little. "Ohio. A Yankee girl."

"She just new come, Mr. Daley. She still getting used to our ways."

"Yes. Well. She's very pretty, isn't she? Thought Yankee women looked a little different. What cause you to come down here?"

"I'm the teacher at the new Milford school. Sir." Mandy added the title for respect, he guessed, but it sounded far from respectful to him.

"I heard talk about a new school over there. Don't even have one in Crumpton."

"I can contact the American Missionary Society or my old college if you'd like to help."

Still on his arm, she hadn't moved from his side, but her overall way was so forward, so brash. She didn't even know it. *Help us, God.*

"That would be nice, honey. I was talking about a school for our white children here."

"The Missionary Society starts schools for all children. Sir. Doesn't matter the color."

"That so? Most interesting. Mrs. Milford know this?"

Virgil patted Mandy's hand. "She the one who sent for her, Mr. Daley. She know."

"I always said Milly had some unusual ideas. If I had known what all her slate ordering was about, I might have done differently."

"But we appreciate you helping us. Sir." Mandy's eyes looked straight ahead, appearing as if she inspected the goods just behind Mr. Daley's shoulders.

"I see. What are you in here for? Got something good to trade me for, Virgil? Virgil's a good boy. Always trades in quality goods."

Virgil bristled at this reference in front of his wife. "Thank you kindly, Mr. Daley. And I always get the goods back." Which wasn't always so. He suspected Daley kept his thumb on the scales whenever something was weighed, but he would be nice today.

"That's right, Virgil. Keep being nice and good things will happen for you. Like you got a pretty wife here. Good things."

"Yes. God's word helps all the time. We going to need flour, salt, a little pack of sugar, nails, and tea."

"Fabric." Mandy pulled on his sleeve. "I want to make a dress for March."

"And for you too." He looked into her eyes, and the light brown glints were back. What a woman he had. What would he do with her?

"Certainly." She let go of his arm and wandered deeper into the back of the store where fabric goods lined the walls in an array of colors and patterns. March followed closely behind, her chin jutting out.

"Mighty high spoken woman there, Virgil."

His comment might have been off the cuff to anyone else, but he read Mr. Daley right. Mandy carried herself too uppity. "She from up north and don't know from down here."

"She need to learn."

"We working on that. Just been married a little more than a week. Sir."

"Very new newlyweds. Well, that's fine Virgil. You deserve some happiness. I hope she makes you happy and doesn't cause any trouble around here."

A cold trickle of sweat slid down the nape of his neck. How had the summer day grown cold so quickly? Must be the morning weather. "Sure enough. Got my staples?"

"Sure enough. And I'm going back here to help your lady fair."

Mandy chose generous lengths of fabric, then pulled money out of her pocket.

Virgil's neck snapped a crick from it, he straightened up so fast. Money? What did she mean to do? "I'll pay for this." Virgil pointed toward his wagon. "Got hams in the wagon for trade

"Virgil cures a fine ham, for sure. But cash money is better."

Why hadn't she discussed this with him before she showed him what she had? Virgil's heart sank at the thought of the merchant having Mandy's money. Money was precious to come by these days and who knew when they would need it? Or how?

They carried the goods to the wagon, and Mandy surveyed the weather-beaten storefronts. "Crumpton's very small."

"Maybe sometime we'll go up to Atlanta, but you got to know how to behave out here." He kept his voice a low whisper. He didn't mean to scold her, but he had to let her know.

"What?" Mandy climbed up onto the wagon box. "What did I do wrong?"

He secured the goods beside the unwanted hams and set March next to them, then hopped up into the wagon box himself. He slapped the reins on the horses' backs, and they set off. Once they were deep in the woods, he exploded at her. "You looked that man in the eyes. You never do that to no man. You're my wife. Keep your eyes low, or you might make him think you interested in him."

"Well, I'm not. I'm your wife. You told him so. Heavens, how strange."

"It's just the way things are done. Ladies, especially Negro ones, got to keep their eyes down."

"Why is that?"

"What did I tell you, Mandy? I'm your husband. I'm telling you for your own protection."

"There's no need to shout at me, Virgil. I can hear."

He cleared his throat. Gracious. "I don't mean to shout at you, Mandy, 'cause you don't know. Those men—they think you interested, they'll come up on you in the road and, and they will get you. Take you." He lowered his voice, hoping March wouldn't hear, but he needed to make his meaning clear. Now. "They take you in God's way. Like a husband s'posed to take his wife."

The light brown glints dissolved in the horror in her eyes. "That was in slavery. Not now, Virgil."

"Bad times ain't that long ago. We don't know what they still do, what not. Ain't trying to test them. I'm just telling you, so you know. I'm your husband now, and you do as I say."

"But not my for real husband."

He pulled up the reins short, stilling the horses to make sure he heard her right.

"We are for sure married by legal way. I'm your husband, woman."

"Oh, yes." Mandy fanned herself against the heat of the day. "But there is another way husbands and wives belong to each other. God's way. You just said so yourself."

Horror shot through his veins like icy water. Before God, what would he do with this woman who was smarter than he was?

CHAPTER TWELVE

Her husband's back stayed rigid in the brown broadcloth he wore. "Got to visit Mrs. Milford before we head on back to the schoolhouse."

"Do you think we'll have time?"

Virgil stared at her as if she had three heads. "We been in town; we need to make the time to see her. Let her know what's going on. She ain't so spry these days, and she love to know."

"But is it all right, if she's not expecting us?"

"Milford ain't Oberlin. We don't have to be proper all of the time." He turned from her.

"I just want to make sure. I don't want to agitate her."

"March here," he said in his stern, deep voice, "is going to have to still herself, keep all of them legs and things from moving. But I know she can do that, right, little girl?"

"Of course, Papa."

"Won't do for you to be too bold, little miss. Just *yes* will do fine."

"Yes, Papa."

If it had been in her purview to call on the Lord in vain, she might have done so at this wearisome exchange. As it was, she jounced along in the wagon as it rolled along an unfamiliar road.

When they arrived, Virgil tied up the horses and got March to stay still and quiet in the back of the wagon. Why couldn't March come with them? Why did Virgil always keep March separate from Mrs. Milford?

It was fine to be her mother, feed her, school her, and make her a dress. But this whole question of why March could be here but not there? Well, that was just a mystery. One she would keep her attention on.

Charles, the butler, greeted them again and told them Mrs. Milford was still in bed. Worry etched deep into Charles's smooth brown features, and Amanda's heart went out to him.

Virgil shook his head. "I thought she wasn't feeling good. Here it is in the middle of the day. She ought to be up and about and she's still abed."

Her husband's handsome face contorted with his concern. More mystery. Still, she laid an arm on Virgil's and spoke to the butler. "Would it be okay if I went to visit?"

Charles's eyebrows shot up as if in shock. "I'll ask her," he said and departed from them.

Was that wrong? She shrugged her shoulders and faced Virgil. "Well, one of us should go in."

"Mandy, why are you so forward? Didn't your daddy tell you how to be?"

She regarded him evenly. "Not in that way."

"Do God."

"I've put my hand to the plow and I won't go back now."

She had him. He opened his mouth to respond, but the butler gestured from the top of the stairs. "She wants to see you both."

Virgil hung back, but the butler waved them forward. She put her arm through Virgil's. He did not move one inch. "I ain't never been in no white lady's bedroom, and I'm not looking to go to one now."

"She invited you to come. I'm here and the butler is here. We could have brought March in…"

"No!" Virgil's whisper echoed throughout the house which, despite its largeness, was quite homely looking and empty. Her fingers itched at the thought of what she could do if given half a chance, but maybe Mrs. Milford was not a decorating kind of lady.

They climbed the rickety stairs, and the toll the war had taken on the home saddened Amanda. The frayed carpet showed that Milford plantation had been used by Union soldiers as a place to stay. It had only been spared fire because of Mrs. Milford's birth in New York state.

Virgil's arm tensed. Although her hand felt small on his bulging muscles, she patted him there a bit so he would calm down. But he hardly seemed aware of what she was doing.

"Wait here," Charles directed them, then opened a door.

Virgil's eyes bore into hers as they stood in the hallway, as if he asked her what she meant by patting him. She just smiled at him and, when the butler waved to them, stood by his side as they glided into the room. After all, if Virgil were to be a great mayor, he needed to get used to uncomfortable situations.

That's why she was there to help him.

He knew where the outhouse was if he needed it.

The thought made him feel better. But what was really helping him enter the forbidden chamber of a white woman's bedroom was Mandy on his arm. The swing of her skirt next to his pants leg made a quiet and pleasant swishing noise, and the motion tickled his leg—'cept he wasn't ticklish. It just felt nice.

Millicent Milford sat up in bed with her gray hair in two long plaits. Her face was sunken in, and her skin was sallow-colored. Virgil's heart slammed in his chest, despite what he wanted to feel. And what was that? Anger? Laughter? Sorrow? Joy? All of them mixed up?

Yeah, it was clear the old lady was on her deathbed. *Please, God. Help me say what's right.*

Part of that meant forgiveness for Sally and March, but he didn't know if he was willing to do that or not.

Mandy spoke first. "Good afternoon, Mrs. Milford."

"Amanda. Lovely frock you have on."

"Thank you, ma'am. It was one of the few I didn't sell before I came down here."

Virgil's arm tightened. Did Mandy even know what she was saying? He looked down at her pleasant face. Nope. She was as placid and calm as ever. No, she didn't know. But then she gave him a little squeeze. Her touch echoed throughout the brown broadcloth, and his knees felt just a little bit stronger.

"Virgil, I declare. You look like a long-tailed cat in a room full of rocking chairs."

"Never been in a woman's bedroom, ma'am."

"I know. You're just so proper and upstanding. If you weren't so bent on doing the right thing all the time, you'd have been in plenty of women's bedrooms."

Her cackle echoed throughout the room, but there wasn't nothing funny about it. This here room, her bedroom, was Sally's torture chamber. That's all he knew. Now he stood in here with his new wife. All of his feelings came together in his stomach and swirled in there something awful.

Mandy gave a little laugh beside him. She was young and knew nothing about the past. Instead of feeling bad, he grabbed her little arm a bit harder, and it gave him strength. If he had anything to say about it, she wouldn't need to know nothing. It was his job to protect this tiny, and by the grace of God, he would do it.

"I'm sorry you have to be here, Virgil. Not feeling too good these days. I just need to be here in this bed, you understand."

"Yes, ma'am. And we didn't warn you we was coming past."

"No, you didn't."

Mandy squeezed his arm back, and he wanted to smile. A little. So she'd been right. He spoke. "Just got back from town. Letting you know the happenings."

"Happenings?" Mrs. Milford shifted and sat up a little more.

"Just the storekeeper. I let him know about the school out here. Wasn't too happy about it."

"Hmm. I would have suspected that. There's no school in Crumpton to teach the young whites."

"No, ma'am."

"You there. Amanda. Can a school be gotten up?"

"I'm happy to write to Oberlin or the Missionary Society to see if any of my schoolmates are available."

"Are they white?"

Mandy's dimples deepened, and for a second, his palms sweated for her. Why did she have to answer that kind of question?

"I've got to know, child. Can't have someone like you teaching the white children. That's all."

"Most of my schoolmates were white, ma'am." Mandy slipped from his armhold and picked up a pillow beside Mrs. Milford and fluffed it.

"I see. I didn't know what kind of school this Oberlin was, that someone like yourself should come out of it."

"The school opened to Negro students about thirty years ago. My father graduated in one of those first classes."

"Was he a slave?"

"No, ma'am. He was a free man. My mother was a slave."

Virgil turned and looked at the top of her head. He hadn't realized that. She was just like March. No wonder they had a special bond between them.

"What was she doing in Ohio?"

"She had escaped."

"Oh, my. I had a slave run away up north. Just once. Took a powerful long time to track her down. Mr. Milford sold her. She was trouble."

"That seems to be how it worked. My father hid her, then bought her freedom from her owner. He educated her, and she learned well. She might have attended Oberlin herself, but they fell in love and she opted to marry him instead. She made him promise to educate me, though."

"Ah, promises. That's important, isn't it, Virgil? To keep promises."

"Sure enough."

"And we can see your father did well, my dear. Write to your white classmates to see if someone can teach in Crumpton. We don't want them getting all preoccupied with the fact that there's something here that they don't have."

"I agree." Mandy withdrew from fluffing the pillows and stood next to him again. He felt better with her by his side. "Although it would seem to make sense for the school to be at a more central location than right next door. If it were in a more central place, then more of the Crumpton children could attend."

"You have thoroughly Northern sensibilities, Amanda. They wouldn't send their children to be taught by you, even if most of the parents can't read and write themselves. No. Best to get Crumpton a teacher of their own. I'll help fund it." Mrs. Milford bent, coughing.

Virgil stayed where he was.

"That all the report, Virgil?"

"It's enough for today, ma'am. You don't seem as if you up to more."

"Don't let me fool you. I'll be fine. I'm pulling through this."

"You'll outlive us all, ma'am." Virgil grasped Mandy's hand and tucked it back into the crook of his arm. She seemed a little surprised.

So was he, to tell the truth. Touching Mandy's cool, calm, steady hand gave him more strength to endure this strange time in this woman's bedroom.

"No more sass, Virgil. I daresay you'll be glad to see me go."

"Didn't say any of that, Mrs. Milford."

"If I wasn't here, you wouldn't have to be reporting to me up in my bedroom, is that it? You could be enjoying being with your new wife here, enjoying March." Mrs. Milford pulled herself up a bit. "Where's March?"

"Outside, ma'am. She dirty and shouldn't be in your clean house."

"She's such a sweet child, though."

"Maybe next time, ma'am." He kept his voice beyond respectful, so she wouldn't be able to say that he sassed her in any way. But she knew.

So did he. It was a dangerous game he played.

Mandy knew nothing of this.

"I have plans for that child."

"I've heard you say, ma'am."

"You don't agree, Virgil. Don't patronize me. I can tell."

"I don't know what you mean, ma'am."

Mrs. Milford wagged her finger at him. "Yes, you do. For all it was hard to teach you to read, you know what I'm talking about."

"Yes, ma'am."

Mrs. Milford looked at Mandy. "You teaching him now?"

A puddle on the floor. That's all he was.

Mandy smiled. "Virgil has great intelligence. He's getting started and is doing very well."

What did she say?

"Lord knows I tried to teach him. Failed. One of my big failures."

"Some people learn in a different way, ma'am. I recall one of my father's pupils in the law who needed to speak aloud. We would just shut him away in a room. But he was very bright and is beginning a law practice of his own."

"Isn't that something? Shouldn't have given up on you so easily, Virgil."

"I've been fine, ma'am."

"No doubt of that. He has a good heart, this one here. You going to Milledgeville for me?"

"Don't see no sense in doing that, ma'am."

Mrs. Milford struck a weak fist against the bedclothes. "This is a time of change. You need to be in the capital to see where men like you are needed. Men, both black and white, respect you. Doesn't happen often. It's rare."

"It is indeed." Mandy moved her hand closer to his. Was she going to clench her hand in his? No. She stopped just short at the end of his sleeve. A wave of emotion overwhelmed him. She hadn't laced her long, tapering fingers through his. What would that feel like? Her soft skin in his hand would make enduring this painful visit worthwhile.

"Don't rightly know."

"Eh. I thought when you got this wife here of yours you might have gotten some better sense about it."

"Yes, ma'am."

"Well, I'm tired. If there isn't any more town gossip for you to say."

Busy little footsteps beat a drum-like tattoo down the hallway Virgil's heart began to pound, faster. He turned to the doorway, and a little face appeared there. March.

His heart sank into his shoes. Why didn't his own child listen to him?

That tiny Mandy—she brought this… this… disobedience into his life. He would stop this once and for all.

"March, I done told you to stay in the wagon."

Virgil fairly quivered in anger beside Amanda. Why?

"There she is," Mrs. Milford said. "Why you aren't the least bit dirty at all. Come on here, child."

March hesitated and hovered in the doorway. She didn't seem to know what to do. How strange. Had March ever stayed still in one place for so long?

Virgil's eyebrows became one in the middle of his forehead, the very picture of an angry deity. He provided such a sharp contrast to the weak, frail, white Mrs. Milford, the proverbial night and day.

Someone had to end this impasse.

It ripped her apart in her middle, but she left Virgil's side and went to March in the doorway. She took her by the hand. "Mrs. Milford isn't feeling well, March. We can't disturb her for a long period of time. She's tired and needs her rest."

"Let me see the dear child. Bring her on here."

What was the harm in it? She guided March to Mrs. Milford's bedside. "Be gentle, March. When someone isn't well, a body feels hurt. So be careful."

March sat her little body down next to Mrs. Milford, and the frail woman lifted her arm up to embrace the child. "Mercy, she's the image of my Sally."

Virgil stepped forward. "We got to go. Don't want to take up any more of your time."

"Virgil, I—"

"Mrs. Milford. We stay long enough. Me and my family be getting on now. Good day."

All the starch and joy seemed to retreat from the woman. She faced Virgil who was gripping the bedpost so hard, he seemed as if he would break it in two. "We don't want to wear you out, ma'am. We'll get along and visit another day."

"That might be best." Mrs. Milford ran a hand over March's braids and grasped her hand, bony hand to bony hand.

Amanda gently tugged March off of the bed.

Mrs. Milford watched them go. "I don't have the strength to fight anymore."

Fight? What was there to fight about? "Of course, ma'am. Take your rest."

"Did you mean what you said just now? About visiting another day?"

Virgil left from the room. He had not even said a proper goodbye. Amanda forced a smile for Mrs. Milford. "I'll be glad to come, if my husband will let me."

Mrs. Milford's blue eyes filled with tears. "You must obey your wedding vows, child. Virgil may not let you come. I understand that. I pray to God that he forgives me for what I've done."

What had happened?

She wanted to ask more, but the old woman fell back on her pillows. Taking March by the hand, Amanda retreated from the room and went down the stairs to the wagon.

Virgil perched up high on the seat, the horses' reins in hand. March clambered into the back of the wagon, and he extended his hand to Amanda to help her up. No lifting up. Her heart sank in disappointment at not having Virgil's strong hands wrap around her waist. She'd barely settled before he slapped the reins and they were off.

Virgil spoke to March over his shoulder. "Next time you don't listen to what I say, you get a tree branch to your bottom."

"Yes, Papa." March's small body cowered in the back.

She had to speak. "Virgil, is that called for? March didn't do anything."

"She disobeyed me. You showed her how when you disobeyed me in the store this morning."

"Well, I'm not March."

"But you're my wife and you need to do as I say."

She swallowed a lump in her throat. "May I ask what is so wrong about visiting an old lady? Or is that a way to disobey you as well?"

"Mrs. Milford isn't just some old lady. She owned us, body and soul, until I bought myself away and she…"

"She what?"

Emotion contorted his face. The sight alarmed her so, she clenched at her skirts to prepare herself, ready to hear what he would say but afraid to hear it at the same time.

He struggled to get the words out. "She sold my Sally away. She sold March's mother away to pay for knickknacks in her house, and my March ain't never seen her mother nevermore. That's why."

Tears smarted in her eyes. "I'm sorry. I didn't know. I just thought—"

"That's why you got to trust me. You being up north, you don't know what it is down here. You don't know nothing about us."

How could she know if he wouldn't talk to her? So much secrecy. Her hot tears fell at his revelation. This was what her father had spoken of, the pain of slavery on both sides in ripping apart family bonds and destroying the souls of owners. The truth of her father's words made her miss him all the more. She hugged herself as the wagon took them home.

Just as her father would have hugged her.

CHAPTER THIRTEEN

Her stomach quaked all afternoon. Could she convince Virgil how sorry she was?

Her father had warned her that she needed to be more prudent. She offended Virgil at nearly every turn—making his daughter a black dress, throwing herself upon him in attempts to get a kiss, and now this. What kind of teacher was she if she could not do the most basic thing and see from more than one point of view?

When they rode up to the schoolhouse and the adult students were waving her in, a lump rose in her throat. Maybe she was needed here. Maybe she could do some good for these people. The horses clip-clopped her to the front door, and Virgil let her down as a gentleman would. He spoke with a few of the adults but stayed firmly ensconced on the wagon seat. Would he come down and be a part of the Saturday school?

Why wouldn't he? His progress would be as any other student, step by step, but still he resisted showing his true self to his town population. And to her.

Never to her, the impulsive Amanda. Who was, to be sure, nothing like the slow and steady hand of Sally.

Her heart throbbed in pain when she thought of Sally having been sold away from her child, sold away from her brothers and sisters and those she loved—for what Mrs. Milford wanted to possess. Terrible.

That's why she had to make the best of this bad time, teaching Pauline, Isaac, and the others their basic letters. The afternoon flew by, and she dismissed them in time for supper. Cleaning up the schoolroom, she released the fixed smile she wore on her face.

Pauline's voice startled Amanda. "How's married life?"

It wasn't in her to tell an untruth, so she pasted the smile back on her lips. "It will all resolve with God's help. I pray daily."

Pauline threw her head back and laughed. "That bad, hmm?"

Amanda stopped gathering slate pencils. "I didn't mean to sound ungrateful."

"You didn't. I just wonder how somebody put up with Virgil all the time. Sally had a time herself."

"She did?"

"She sure did. He's not a one easy to get along with."

No, he wasn't. But she mustn't complain. Not to anyone. She could be a soiled dove in the clutches of Charles Henry. A knot formed at the back of her throat. She must make a go of this marriage. She just had to. What else existed for her?

"Praying is good. When we was all allowed to get married a few months back, I think people thought everything was going to be milk and honey."

People generally did think that about marriage. "And?" Amanda gulped.

"Just like everything else in life. Lot of hard work."

"I think he misses Sally a great deal, so it's hard to be in her place and not be her. Such disappointment he must feel."

Pauline laid a hand on her shoulder. "That's not it at all. I'm not saying he don't miss Sally. I'm just saying this is different for him, 'cause you a different woman. He don't want to disappoint you, 'cause you're smart and educated. That's a big thing for a man. Anytime a woman got something a man don't—it was hard for Isaac at first too. He younger than me. I got my own house. Took him a bit to find his place in it. I figure every new situation needs time to get used to."

Pauline made complete sense there.

"You all was called to come together when you didn't even know one another. So you takes the time you need to get to know him and for him to know you. Meantime, you be here at this school and we are grateful, even if he ain't, because we need you. You doing good."

"Thank you. I appreciate it. I have to start dinner now."

Pauline chuckled deep in her throat. "Don't let all his rumbling get to you. He's a big old softie deep down in his soul. But I'll be praying for you too."

"Thank you."

Walking up the hill, Amanda reflected on all Pauline had shared. Maybe she needed to know more about Sally to be a full wife to Virgil, but really she needed to focus on the relationship between them. Starting with apologizing and trusting more in what he said.

When she went into the house, March was setting silverware on the table and pushed forward a tin pot full of wildflowers she'd picked. The flowers bent over a bit, but their heady fragrance and color brightened up the table and her spirits. Amanda hugged the girl to her. "Thank you for that, honey."

"Papa told me to start up the supper fixings. Said you might be hungry after such a long day."

"Where's your papa?"

"Out in the barn."

"Keep setting the table. I'll be back presently to help with the ham steaks. Don't let the beans burn."

"Yes, Mamma." March nodded her head and sang a little ditty to herself as she worked.

Amanda found Virgil mucking out the horses' stalls. A thankless boring task to be sure, but one she knew was necessary to keep a horse's shoes in pristine condition.

She folded her arms over herself to keep her emotions in check. "Missed you at the Saturday school."

"Not going into that schoolhouse while other folk is there."

"You don't think of it as an opportunity to set a good example?"

"No. Take me longer than everyone else to learn. People see I ain't fit to be the mayor and run me out of the office."

"Oh, Virgil. Why are you so hard on yourself?"

"And who are you to be saying such things?"

"I'm your wife, if you've forgotten."

He turned to adjust a harness, then spoke. "No. Haven't forgotten. Can't forget."

What did that mean? How sorry he was to be saddled with her for the rest of his life? Well, she was too. What about what she felt? "Fine then. We have to make the best of this situation."

"Doing what I can."

"As am I."

He stopped his mucking. "Sometimes lessons aren't just in books."

"I'm fully aware of that."

"I'm your husband."

"I understand that as well." She rubbed her arms to warm herself.

"You need to trust me when I say do."

"Sometimes I feel…"

Virgil put down his pitchfork and stepped closer. He wore his informal clothes today and had been working hard. His manly scent of sweat and horses mixed together clouded her mind. He had a fine sheen of sweat on his face, and his eyebrows drew together in displeasure. He took her by the arm. "Sometimes it's about what's in here." He took her hand and placed it on his chest. "Right here. There's a feeling here says *danger*."

The hardness of his chest caused her hand to almost bounce off. She cleared her throat. "Of course. There's always conflict between the head and the heart."

"Then that's you and me. You the head. I'm the heart. Sometimes you got to trust the heart."

Oh my. The heart. The seat of all that was emotional and unsure. Hers was surely pounding up now. "I see."

"I wonder what you see up in that educated mind of yours. Everything don't work out as it do in books."

"And you know that because you've read them?"

He dropped her hand, and cold air closed in about her again. She opened her lips to apologize, but Virgil waved her away. He beckoned her away with his eyes. No apologies. "You need to see what March is up to, trying to make the dinner."

"Of course."

She stepped away, wanting to be the first one to leave the confrontation, the first one in the house. And she was. The winner. What a feeling of joy at that victory.

No, it was all emptiness.

She sliced off several ham steaks from a shank. One they hadn't been able to use in trade because of her interference. Was there knowledge that could not be easily attained by reading? How much did Virgil have to teach her? She sensed by today's events that she was just a babe in the woods. Is that how he felt when she was teaching him?

How she wished she had paid better attention when her father told her how the enslaved had suffered in the South. There was so much wisdom in his diaries.

Virgil had a different kind of knowledge that demanded respect too. She needed to position herself to learn. He had done the same for her. She could do no less for him.

"Good night, Daddy."

He looked forward to this time of day when March went to bed. Her little red scarf tied down her braids to keep them smooth while she slept, wild, in her cot bed. Mandy had taken apart an old Milford granddaughter's dress and made it into a suitable nightgown. When she wasn't cooking or teaching, Mandy's head, heavy with her looped-up braids, would be bent to her sewing, always creating something for March.

Still, agreeing to this marriage was like going back to old times. Really, he was just doing what Mrs. Milford said do, and why? To make him feel better that she had stolen his wife, sold her down river? Something she said she would never do?

No. It was for March. March needed a mamma. As much as he hated to admit it, March needed a new dress. He coulda went and bought his own child a dress out of the store, but sometimes that was tricky. No, it was better to go about it like Mandy did, go in the back of the store and get bolts of cloth and make your own. Sewing was a good skill for a girl to have, and he couldn't have taught her that. Pauline would do her braids, but March's hair looked much better in Mandy's care. She was smoothed out. She ate more. She even tried to stay still. Some of the time.

His daughter's constant fidgeting made him smile inside. March moved as if she had fire dancing through her fingers. She was born at a good time, right as the bad times ended so she wouldn't have all of that beaten—or worse—out of her.

Even if Mrs. Milford still looked at March with desirable eyes.

What else would March be able to do with herself but be Mrs. Milford's maid, just as her mother was? Six was the right age to be taken into the house and taught a few chores to help out. All of this making him mayor, asking him to run for political office and such, helped Mrs. Milford get close to his daughter. She'd snatch her up into that big house when he was gone on a trip or wasn't looking.

Miss Lady Mandy, her whole perspective would be that it was okay, like Mrs. Milford was just an old lady looking for company.

'Cepting she wasn't, and he knew it and so did Mrs. Milford. Mandy and March were the only two who didn't know.

Could March be a teacher? Seemed a better choice for his daughter, yet, until recently, so far away a possibility that it would have been laughable.

Until Mandy Stewart came into their lives. Mandy Smithson.

She entered the living room with her skirts swishing about her. She stood in front of him after the turmoil they'd faced today. "Are you ready?"

"Could ask you the same, it seems to me."

She let out a breath and put her hands in her skirt pockets. Must have liked pockets in her skirt. Smart as she was with a needle, it would be no problem to make up pockets. "I apologize. I honestly do. Here."

With a swift motion, she pushed his feet off the footstool and sat on it, her brown plaid skirts arranged about her. Not in the big cascading way they'd been on the very first day he'd seen her, but still pleasing. She situated herself on the footstool and faced him.

"What are you doing, woman?"

"I'm showing you I'm ready to learn. It's more than you are doing now, since you ought to be in at the table, learning the next letter."

"I was coming."

"Oh, no. You should have been there as I took March up to bed. No, you stayed in here and wanted to pout because I made mistakes today."

"I'm a man fully grown. No need for pouting."

"Well, good. Get on in there and start practicing on the slate. But one thing before you go."

He eased to the edge of his chair, ready to away to where the biggest kerosene lamp waited. "What is it?"

"Tell me one thing about Sally."

"No need of you going to pry into other folks business."

"You said I don't know anything. Maybe you should start schooling me."

Why did she have to make so much sense for a person so tiny? She sat there, chin perched on her hands, staring straight at him. She thrust a leg out across from his. Rascal. A little expanse of smooth brown leg poked out from the edge of her high top shoe.

His mouth felt dry. "Don't have nothing to say."

She didn't move. "One thing. If you want, look on it as my pay for teaching you letters."

He gripped the edges of the chair. What to tell her? Something that didn't mean anything. Something small. Something insignificant. "There was some other man over to Crumpton what wanted Sally for himself. I had to wrassle him to show him who was boss."

"Let me understand this. You're a blacksmith. You preach beautiful, fiery oratory. Now you're the town mayor. And you wrassled a man to show you were the better provider to Sally?" Shoulders slumped, she pulled her hands out of her pockets to cover her mouth in a girlish giggle.

"What you laughing about?"

"You always are so buttoned up and serious. I cannot imagine you wrassling for anything."

He leaned down and brought his face closer to hers. He only wanted to make his point, but instead he got pulled into her eyes—those dark black eyes—and searched for the hazel glints. "I'm willing to fight for what I want."

The glints danced out of her eyes and went elsewhere. He surely didn't mean to scare her, so he started to pull back, but then she leaned in even closer.

Do Lord. What was she going to do now?

She breathed in, out, that faint orange smell of hers circling him. Finally she spoke. "Then go fight with that slate and make those letters what they need to be."

She stood up, taller than him for just a second, and put her hands on her hips. "I think *k* is next."

He stood up too, only now aware that they were in each other's space. He breathed out a bit to steady his rapidly beating heart. "The sound."

"Kay. Kay. Kay." Her pink lips slightly parted, and the sound came from her throat.

Was she trying to be a torment, as Eve was to Adam in the garden of Eden with her pink lips all parted up like that?

"Say it now. Kay. Kay."

No, she wasn't trying to be a torment. She was trying to get him to the lesson. Just as she said. "Kay. Kay. Kay."

"Very good."

He turned and tried to go past her. Her small hand on his arm—his bare arm since he'd rolled up his sleeve—stopped him. *Do Lord.*

"Thank you for telling me about Sally."

"You welcome. Best go on in before the light goes out."

"I just know it's hard when you lose a loved one. I lost my mother when I was young and now my father… I miss him."

He lightly laid a hand on her elbow. "You had a father. He taught you many things, and that's wonderful. Didn't have time to teach you everything, though. That's what I'm here for."

A slow, sly smile crawled across her face. "So you will be a father to me?"

He cleared his throat, not sure what she meant by that smile. "I try to help anyone in the world. You just said you're an orphan. I'm here to help."

"I'm an adult orphan who is also your wife."

"Well, yes. And I'm here to help you in any way I can."

There went her small, strong hands in the pockets again. "I see. Well, best get in to the room."

"Yes. Afore the light goes."

He allowed her to step in front of him. When she did, he couldn't stop himself, couldn't help it. His hand stole to the small of her back to guide her in. Her tiny waist was so enticing, calling him to support her.

She turned to him and showed her dimples, gesturing with her arm to the learning table.

Everything swirled about in his head so that he didn't know who was the teacher and who the student.

Everything all mixed up.

Chapter Fourteen

Virgil didn't know how to bring up the next subject. Nothing to do but just say it.

So, a few weeks later, when they waved goodbye to the last parishioner after church service, they started the walk back to their home for Sunday dinner.

Now was the time to say what was on his mine. He turned to his wife and took in a sharp breath. "If you want me to go to Milledgeville on mayor business, you going to have to learn how to protect yourself here."

She frowned at him. "Protect myself?"

"Yes, and March. I can't be going off to the capital, leaving you on top of this hill without protection."

"Everyone knows I'm your wife. Why would any harm come to me?"

What kind of life had Mandy lived afore she came to Milford? Seem to be on the moon or something, never having to worry about your own safety. "Not everyone loves me, Mandy."

She made a funny face, scrunching up her nose. Even her dimples showed up to the party. "Well, I don't know. There are plenty of tittering young women who love to hear you preach. Plenty more older ladies too. Men look up to you and see Virgil

Smithson, the mayor, strutting about." That scamp started to walk around, squaring her shoulders up, looking just like him.

March galloped into the room, saw what her mamma did, and started walking like that too, laughing with her.

Laughter bubbled up inside of him, but he squelched it down. Wouldn't do to have March see him being so frivolous. Somebody had to be the grown-up in this family. "You all cut that out now."

Mandy cast aside the persona she wore and grew serious again. "What do I need to do?"

"Learn how to shoot off my rifle."

"A rifle?"

"Yes, Mrs. Smithson. Got to learn how to shoot. We go outside now, and get some target practice up. Don't have to leave yet for a few more weeks, but we make sure by the time I go, you can protect the home."

"Okay." Mandy shrugged her shoulders, and she and March stared at each other. He pulled up his suspenders from where they'd been dangling post–sermon, relaxing after one of Mandy's good dinners of beef, beans, and potatoes. Grape pie too. Some good.

They walked out behind the house, high on the bluff of the hill with all of Milford proper below them. Mrs. Milford's big white house was a faint white blur against the blue sky. "March, go on back and get some tin cans out my tin pile. Take care you don't cut yourself." Wouldn't do no harm to shoot them up. They could go right back in his pile later.

March ran to do his bidding. Virgil tossed the gun to her and she caught it in both hands, almost pulling her down. "Got to stand up with a gun."

"I will. I just—you startled me with it. Well, Virgil, you practically threw it at me. And you have to be careful with a gun. My mother was shot by accident once."

"I apologize. Thought you was ready was all."

March came running out with four cans, two in each hand, holding the bottoms so she wouldn't get cut.

"Put them on that log over there."

"Like this, Daddy?"

"Spread them out more. That's fine. Get on back here now." Wouldn't hurt March to watch this lesson with her mother. She would need this information someday.

"Thing about the rifle is, you got to be ready for the kickback. You not ready, a tiny like you could get knocked flat on the ground and hurt yourself. Maybe others too if the gun go off who knows where. Got to be responsible for your ammunition."

"Yes." Her voice seemed a little stirred up. *Please, God, help her learn*. He couldn't imagine leaving once more without his woman being protected. Not like last time. No more Sallys in his life. He'd had enough.

"You all right?"

"The rifle is very large."

"It be my rifle. And I'm a large man. Need a large gun."

"Oh." The hazel glints danced again in her eyes.

Best to ignore that and be about business. "Hold it up on your shoulder."

She tried to gather all of the gun up on her, but she was, as he'd been saying all along, a tiny.

"Maybe Mamma needs her own gun."

Not a bad idea, but they needed to try the rifle first.

"Hold it like this." Virgil came behind her and surrounded her with his arms. "I'm sorry, but there's no other way to show you how to hold it right."

"I see. It's all right."

His big arms encircled Mandy's head. He shifted himself a tad lower so his arms were right next to hers. He positioned her small hands on the rifle. "Here, now you in an aiming place. Go on ahead and see if you can get that first can knocked off. Squeeze it gentle now."

He kept his arms around her so the recoil wouldn't make her flinch. Mandy pulled the trigger, and the can shot off cleanly.

"Yay, Mamma!" March cried behind them.

"That was good," he said grudgingly. After all, he had helped her. He removed his arms from around her body. Too bad he couldn't linger a little longer, inhaling the orange scent of her hair.

"Good?" Mandy leveled the rifle up on her shoulder.

The charmed dimple look was gone. She changed into a determined focused woman, someone he didn't know, and shot the cans off the log with three clean shots.

March stood next to him, and both of their jaws dropped in shock. "Well." His throat worked against him, staying dry and hard. "You sure showed us."

"Great shooting, Mamma."

March handed him the rifle.

The laughter fair bubbled from her, and the dimples came out. "I'm sorry, Virgil. We have guns in Ohio. You worked with the Union Army as I recall. Surely you would know that."

"Your papa teach you?"

"Yes. He had to go on trips sometimes and wanted me to know how to protect myself. Same as you. So I guess you two are alike in more than one way." She swallowed and looked toward the cans. "The one thing he didn't protect me from was Charles Henry."

The hazel glints left whenever she spoke about that man. Virgil wanted to get on a train and go up to Ohio, find that man, and tell him a thing or two. Then stop off to Lawrence Stewart's gravesite and say a few words there. "Well, then, I will be less afraid to go. But you've got to promise me that you don't go looking for confrontation. Sometimes, when you are down here, the best thing is to turn the other cheek."

She fixed her hands on her hips. "Well, listen to the preacher."

"I mean what I say."

"And you wouldn't be a preacher if you didn't." Mandy reached up and touched his cheek, meaning to tap him, he guessed. But he didn't like her trying to be funny about something serious. He meant what he said, and this woman sometimes didn't seem to catch his meaning. He caught her by the wrist, and she took a deep breath in, so sharp he could hear it whistling in her lungs.

"I been through a loss one time afore. Not going through it again."

She made a small fist of her hand. "Oh, Virgil. Life is all about loss. We learn how to deal with it."

He let her go. Yeah, he'd told her more about Sally as he'd learned lessons from her. But Mandy had not been there. Not enough to know. He released her hand and bent for his bullets. "Like with your daddy?"

"Yes. A bit. But he will always be with me because he helped me learn how to shoot. I learned the lesson."

He turned swiftly to see if she were joking.

Her posture was completely serious.

Taking the rifle, he stomped back into the house. A remarkable woman he had married, for sure. Was there anything, something, that she didn't know how to do? Almost make him believe she didn't need him at all.

Now he understood. He was the one who needed her.

How could Amanda fit into this family? Could Virgil need her as much as she needed him?

"Good." He finished the last of the grape pie. "How you figure that out?"

She wiped down the table with a rag. "March showed me some of God's bounty down here. These big juicy grapes." She showed him the size of the grape with her fingers.

"Never saw the like in Ohio."

"No. Seems to be something from down 'round here. Folks call them *scadies*. Name's muscadine."

"*Scadies*, that's what March called them. She'd been eating a bunch and gave me some, so I wasn't afraid. I knew about grape pie growing up, so I gave it a try with these big, big fruits. It's not quite the same, but it came out well. They probably make good jelly too."

"Jelly's good. Can take some in to Crumpton to sell if you like. Give you a little pin money."

"I don't know that I need pin money besides what the school pays me."

"Still. Good for a woman to have money of her own."

What for? In case she decided to run off and live a life of her own?

She was here. He still didn't seem to understand that. She had taken vows before God to be here, to be part of his life and March's life.

To her surprise, Virgil started to chuckle low in his throat. A deep, soul-stirring chuckle. "You leave any of them scadies behind on the vines?"

"Yes, I suppose. March gathered up what we needed for the pie."

"If you want to make jelly, better have her get the rest. Although folks 'round here not be happy about it."

"God's bounty is meant to be shared. That's why I told her only to pick what we needed, although she probably ate one for every one in the bucket, throwing away the pips."

"Sure, she did. I'm just thinking some folks be sorry to see them scadies gone a bit. Folks 'round here use them to make wine."

"Wine? Oh, no."

"Yes. Can't afford to buy any, so they makes it out of scadies and other fruit."

"Virgil, you have to stop them from imbibing."

He spread his hands out. "I tell them. A man gets out of hand with his wife sometimes and they get to fighting—I know to blame the scadie wine." He looked up at her, almost smiling.

Was it the pie that made him smile?

"Better send March out to that thicket to get more so's you can make jelly. More jelly, less drinking. Better for all concerned."

"Yes, I think so."

"Mandy." He took her fingertips into his large hand.

She stood there and gulped. The part of her hand not in his began to feel wet. *Please, Lord, don't let my hand be sweaty while he's holding it.*

"Thank you for what you done."

"I'm doing God's work. No need to thank me for that. I'm a servant in his kingdom. Same as you."

"Can't be easy to be married to one such as me."

"I do as I must."

He let her hand drop. Why didn't she know what to say beyond that?

"We all do. 'Scuse me." He walked out, opening the door to the barn and leaving her with the dirty dishes. Again.

"It say," Virgil said the next Sunday to his parishioners, "when a man leaves his mother, and take up a wife, he leave all the childish things behind."

He gripped the podium a bit harder. Whenever he preached in this place, he was always aware of it as Mandy's special place. Sometimes that helped him. Sometimes, it made him feel like he was interfering somehow. "Sometimes, people hears childish. That's not what it really means, though. Means to leave behind what is comfortable and familiar. When you get to be big, you got to put away what you know and reach out for the new. Amen."

"Amen." The crowd echoed.

He glanced at Mandy. One of her dimples came out, and his heart leapt with gladness at the sight of it.

"The new—we all going through some of that now. We knew a time when we had to work for a mistress. Get up a certain time, come to work. Get your rations every year. A bolt of rough cloth. Didn't carry no money."

The room quieted. He knew it was because Mrs. Milford had come up off her bed of affliction to hear him preach again. She claimed it was because she enjoyed it, but he doubted she was as sick as she said she was half the time. That woman would outlive them all.

She liked attention. She especially like the attention of being the only white woman in a schoolhouse full of her former "people," ones who knew no different than to pay attention to her. Well, he had a few things to say about that.

"Our every need was seen to. Except for one." Virgil held up a finger. "We had souls. When President Lincoln wrote up the 'Mancipation papers, that was to free our souls. Praise, God."

"Praise God."

"And seeing to our souls is a different matter. We got to put away what is familiar. We got to go to the new. And it's hard, no matter how long we pray for liberation, to decide for ourselves what is right. It's new. New things are hard.

"Women, they put away the childish too."

"Amen, they does," Pauline called out.

The crowd laughed a bit.

"Maybe you knows I speak about Mrs. Smithson. She get on a train, come down here to Georgia. What she know up there is cold. Pretty hot down here for her."

Mandy held up her fan, and the crowd laughed.

He smiled at her. "She had to leave her papa there in the ground and come into the new. It's not easy for her, God bless her. I know I'm not easy for her. But I thanks her for it, because she did what she had to do. She came away from the familiar to make a new life, to start something else."

"She come to help us all out of the way of ignorance, out of the darkness, to teach our children and even some big folks to the new world of reading and writing and knowing and growing. Amen!"

The spirit had got good to them now, probably 'cause he was shouting and waving his arms. He loved this part of the preaching. "Praise God, she such a brave tiny."

People quieted and chuckled. "A brave one. She show me the way. She asked me. Maybe she told me?"

"Told!" Pauline shouted, causing more laughter. He smiled and held up a hand. Folks quieted down, seeing that he was serious.

"Been asked to take up something new. Seems like they wants people who look like us up in the state house now. No one surprised 'bout that more than me. But it's a new day. And I'm going up. I be leaving for Milledgeville on mayor business in the next day or two."

At first there was silence. Then the crowd applauded. "Praise God. Praise him!"

Was that Pauline who had tears shining on her cheeks? Do God. He never seen her cry.

He waited until they quieted again. "Ain't saying I ain't afraid. Might be plenty to be scared of, something I don't know. But I'm saying we all got to do it. We all got to try. We all have to grow. We all have to help our people along to a new day. We all have work to do. Wherever I go, I ain't going nowhere without the people of Milford behind me, amen."

Pauline shot to her feet. "We be there. We going to be there for you, Virgil."

While he loved to stir the people up, when they all popped up to their feet, one by one, no one was more surprised than him.

As usual, Mrs. Milford stepped out of the schoolroom at the pinnacle of the sermon and, on the arm of her most loyal butler, stepped to her carriage.

Virgil looked at Mandy who had stood too. Even in the loud schoolroom, he heard the swish of her brown plaid skirt as she stepped forward and grabbed his hand. "I'm proud of you, Virgil."

"Need to go on ahead and kiss her." Pauline's strong voice rose above the crowd. "You know you want to."

Pauline. Another woman who was a piece of work.

Virgil looked down at Mandy's face, full of hope and expectation. His throat went dry. What if he tried to kiss her and it went horribly wrong in front of all of these people? What if—

Before he knew it, she yanked his hand and pulled him down to her. His lips hovered over hers. She reached out to him. Hadn't thought her pretty pink lips would reach so far, but she closed the gap.

Time to put away childish behavior.

Time to grow on up.

He was married to this woman.

Nothing wrong with slipping into the sweet, pink abyss of her lips touching his. *Do God.*

Tricky thing about doing what Paul said—when you put away childish things and transformed, you were never the same again. That was the very thing he was afraid of.

Because if he lost this, lost her, how in the world would he be able to make it through the rest of his life?

He pulled away. When he saw the tear tracks on her face, he saw himself for the coward he was.

She had fallen in love with him.

He, after he had promised not to, had fallen in love with her.

Dear God. I'ma make this promise. I'm coming back to her. When I come back, I'ma do what I can to make her happy.

Even be her husband in God's way.

Chapter Fifteen

"What do you do to make your garden so lovely?" Amanda and March walked down into the town to visit with Pauline after adult class was over on the next Saturday afternoon. Pauline's disapproval showed in her thinned-out lips. She didn't know why. Pauline's garden was a nice place to be, and Amanda hoped hers would grow as generously whenever she got hers going.

"Horse droppings. Or whatever animal you got. Isaac brings them from the forge." Pauline smiled, watching March jump and dance around. "That's what make things grow. The earth know the earth. And anyone with any sense knows a snake." Pauline sat back on her heels. "Where you going? Virgil don't want you going up to that old woman while he's gone."

"I gathered that. But I sense that she can tell me what I want to know."

"What you want to know?"

"Why is Virgil the way he is? He's so in himself."

"Give him time, honey. Keep making him that good food you making. He come around."

She shook her head. "It's something about me."

Pauline put a hand on her hip. "What about you? You as pretty as a picture and smart to boot. Man coming up in the world like Virgil, going to the capital, leaving my Isaac to watch the town smithy. We been many years down, under the foot of them like her. Jesus say, the first shall be the last and the last first. To me, look like that's what's happening."

"Yes, Pauline. And you should be proud of your husband."

"Oh, yeah. Funny, how we came together. I was always hanging 'round with Sally, and she had this little pesky brother 'round all the time. The most annoying child ever. And he would delight in scaring us."

"Time come, childhood be over. Take up your duties. Sally, she go up to the big house. I stay in the fields. Isaac come in the fields a few years later. That's how I come to know him, better than I know Sally. Sally, she up in that house. Sleeping on the floor in the hallway. Might as well be the moon."

"What was she like?"

"A rose. All folded up."

"A folded-up rose? A rosebud?"

Pauline pointed a finger at her. "That's it. They brung Virgil in, and he was like a bee 'round her rosebud. Wasn't nothing but children theyselves when they got married and had March."

"They were children?"

"Who know? Not allowed to get married back then. Didn't even know how old we was. Old enough for sniffing around one another. We try for things to be proper. So they get married in the yard, take up as man and wife. But Sally's life be up in that house."

"She was busy all the time?"

"Milly, she want her maid to sleep close to her. Mr. Milford ain't there no more. Maid sleep up there, she ain't got no time to sleep next to her own man."

She colored to think of it. "My. That's a shame."

"It was. That's why, time go to the state house, you got to go with him. He's afraid to leave. He has reasons."

Amanda had sent off letters to Ohio a few weeks ago. It would take some time before she heard back from the potential teachers she was thinking of. What if there were ones up there like her? Well, she knew there was. She had a special type of privileged position, living as the daughter of a successful Negro lawyer. She thought of her other classmates, those who were adamant that slavery was a sin but would never think of coming here to teach. Now that she had paved the way, maybe more would come.

She thought back to Pauline's story. "They had March."

"They did. Mrs. Milford, she put a cradle up there for March, so her mamma can stay. Kept all his family from him."

A sharp pain hit her in the chest. Poor Virgil. Was that why he was so reluctant to smile and be happy with her and March?

"Virgil working hard down at the smithy. He a good smith. People come from out of Crumpton—they want Virgil. He came at a very high price when Mr. Milford brought him here. He cost nigh on a thousand dollars."

Amanda wondered at the amazement in Pauline's voice. She had no question, no problem with the fact that Virgil should come at such a price.

"But when he want his freedom, the Milfords say it cost him twice that for him, and another for Sally. Let them have March for free."

"Three thousand dollars."

"That's it, child." Pauline gathered more weeds. "Might as well be the moon. Virgil work hard—what else he going to do? Sally and his baby up in that house all the time. And he get enough to buy himself. A whole pot of money he got."

"Two thousand dollars."

Pauline smiled. "Yes indeed. Virgil some kind of smart to be able to make that kind of money. And he go up there…" Pauline squared her shoulders like Virgil and did a pretty fine impression of him. "He go up there, all that money in his hand. Mr. Milford, he feeling poorly. They needing money and things for his care. And here come Virgil, got two thousand for-sure dollars."

Pauline stopped her tale and wiped her forehead. This woman was strong, physically and in her mind, Amanda could tell. Still, her hesitation showed she was upset. The next part probably wasn't so nice. Amanda squared her shoulders to be ready for it.

"He gave old Frank Milford the money, and Mr. Milford wrote out the freedom papers, and took them to court on top of that to be official. 'Here, Virgil. You free.' Then Virgil say, 'Let me have my family too. Sally work hard. She my wife, and you can trust me for the rest.'"

"Mr. Milford, he mighta done it, if it had just been him. But no. He knew he would have to hear his wife after him about not having her maid where she wanted. Not to mention she had taken a shine to March too."

"My." Amanda swallowed, but the lump in her throat wouldn't go down.

"War and hard times look like it was coming. So they said no. And Mr. Milford say, can't no free people stay here. You got to get out. Can't have you giving the Baxters ideas. One time before, I freed a slave, she had to leave too. So Mr. Milford, he take that money from Virgil, knowing he breaking that family up—something he say he never do. Knowing Virgil can't know different. All a lie."

"Virgil tell Sally, he be back. He go smith somewhere else, tell her he earn that money fast and come back for her and baby

March. I still remembers when he left her up there at the house. A sad time."

Certainly. In her mind's eye, she envisioned a trusting Virgil leaving for other work, only to come back and be disappointed.

"Virgil, when he come back, he tell us he been all over the United States. Had many places where they want him to stay and be their smith. All he wanted was to come back and be with his family. But because of the fighting, money harder to come by. So it took longer. Four whole years."

"My."

"But he got it. One thousand dollars. Brought it to pay them anyway, no matter what Mr. Lincoln said about us being free by then. He come back because that was his word. No one knew what would happen, but by then things looking really bad for the Rebs. And now, he have to deal with Mrs. Milford, cause Mr. Milford dead by then."

"He learn she sold Sally off. To buy things in the house with. Sold her to Alabama. And he promise-- he going to find her."

"Where was March all this time?"

"Mrs. Milford, she try to keep March for herself when she sell Sally, but I went up and got her myself. I says, I'm her auntie. Can't have no babies myself. She don't know nothing about raising no farm child. It was for me to do. Last thing she told me as they taking her to Alabama—take care of March. So I keep her so Virgil could find Sally without having to worry about March."

"But?"

"He find her. She had a big belly since her new master come for her. She was like, what you said, a rosebud. What she going to do? Say no? Cause I'm married to Virgil and I don't know where he is, working for my freedom?"

"What happened?"

"He try to buy her from this new master, but he don't want to sell Sally. He like her too much."

"What did Virgil do?"

"You knows Virgil now. He like a dog with a bone. He ain't giving up, even if this man try to chase him away."

Pauline sniffled. "Time came for Sally to have this master's baby, and she didn't make it."

"She died having the baby?"

Pauline shook her head. "That's what Virgil say."

Amanda shuddered and her shoulders grew cold on the hot day.

Pauline shrugged her shoulders, shaking her head. "He come home and say she died. He held her dead body. He carried her dead body all the way back from Alabama back here to be buried. He say words over her when it come time to bury her. Dug the grave by himself. Wouldn't even let Isaac help."

"And her baby?"

"Died too. March's baby brother. Fix up her body and put the baby in Sally's arms."

March continued her galloping, and Amanda thought of how precious life was and how Sally had struggled so hard to bring forth March and her baby brother. And she died of it. Just a few years older than Amanda was. She hoped that she wouldn't struggle so when it came time for her to have a…

But to have a baby, she would have to be Virgil's wife fully. Completely. And she didn't even know if he cared for her enough. Would that even be possible?

"Such a sad story, Pauline."

"I knows. You coming here provided some happy times again, you know."

"Do you think so?"

"Oh, honey, I know it's true. Virgil come back and swore he would never leave Milford again, 'cause of what happen when he left afore. He done seen enough of the world to know and he don't want any more of it."

Now the way he reacted at Mrs. Milford's offer to go to the state capital made complete sense. *Oh, Virgil. Please, God, help him to attain peace in his mind, heart, body, and soul.*

"Thank you, Pauline." Amanda knew what she had to do, even if it meant disobeying her husband. Given everything he had been through, he didn't deserve a disobedient wife, but if there was a way to make things right for him, she had to try. His tension with Mrs. Milford that kept getting in the way.

Clearing the old hurts with the old mistress might be the only way she could ever have children of her very own. She needed to visit with Mrs. Milford. Today.

For the capital of a state, Milledgeville seemed to have a way to go.

Since the war ended, everything seemed down in the mouth. The capital building was still in poor shape because of Sherman and his men. Everyone was saying that the old capital was done and that there needed to be a better place to have a capital.

Virgil had met other freemen in the boarding house he was staying in. "Been some time since I been in Atlanta," one nattily-dressed freeman said, "but they got a railroad and new buildings there. Might be some better."

He had come to file papers registering him as mayor, but the freemen he'd met were seeking the vote. They talked about seeking office later but were glad to shake his hand—he was living proof of what they thought they could do.

He still didn't understand why they were so excited. These freemen were bold enough to believe they could come to the state house someday, so sure of it that they brought their wives with them, hungry for a seat inside the torn-down Georgia capital building.

What wives they had. Beautiful, graceful ladies--all shades of brown. Mandy's toasty color skin was a shade somewhere in the middle, but she would fit in perfectly. Whether he were called to serve in Milledgeville or elsewhere, she would be ready. What a graceful helpmeet she would be.

Still, his heart hurt to see the people in Milledgeville. Folks here seemed to be far worse off than those in the country. Jobs were scarce, and they didn't own the land to support themselves. If he ever got to the state house, he would make sure he helped these people as well as those back home.

Seemed a heavy burden to carry.

His burden.

Mandy is here to help you carry the burden.

Where had that thought come from? It was surely true, though. He confirmed that when the time came for him to sign where he was listed as mayor of Milford, Georgia. He signed his name, Virgil Smithson, over and over again.

Mandy had taught him that.

There were many who signed *X*'s to the documents. But he signed his name.

Because of Mandy.

The foolishness and waste of his shame came over him as he left the building. He shaded his eyes to see where the sun was. If he rode hard, he would make it.

Instead of staying another day, he got on his horse with the barest of rations and made his way home to tell his wife...

To tell her he'd been a sorry fool. Was it too late? *Dear God, help me with the words. I need her so much.*

"I appreciate you bringing your sewing up, as well as a visit from this young one here." Millicent Milford put her arms around March who willingly hugged the older woman back.

How good to see that Mrs. Milford was out of bed and in a chair in her room. "I have many sewing chores to do, but I also brought the Word of God if it would be a bit of a comfort."

Mrs. Milford laughed. "You're taking your role as a preacher's wife mighty seriously, Amanda."

"I was brought up to do everything with excellence, ma'am."

"A wonderful belief to live by. None of the Bible now, thank you. I'm just enjoying your visit."

"We appreciate it."

"Your husband know you are here?"

"No, ma'am."

"And you aren't afraid of what he might say when he finds out?"

Amanda rested the sprigged cloth on her lap and cut a thread with her scissors. "I don't know if anything of what I do matters much to him."

"Oh now, I would disagree with you there. It always matters."

"He just doesn't like me much."

"I heard about that kiss in church last week, after I left." Mrs. Milford picked up her sewing and pointed something out to March about her own little quilt patch that Amanda had started her on.

"Everyone was there, wanting him to do it. That's why."

Mrs. Milford shook her head. "No. That's not it. I see how he regards you. Virgil, he can be so stubborn, so blind at times.

He doesn't know often what's best for him, right there in front of him."

"So when he purchased his liberty, did he not also purchase the chance to make his own choices?" Her heart beat hard within her. Even if that meant she was one of those choices he had be forced to make...

Amanda watched the emotions that sprang over Mrs. Milford's face. Had the possibility never even occurred to the woman? *Stay by my side, God.* She didn't want to make Mrs. Milford angry. That would be contrary to her purpose.

Mrs. Milford shook her head. "Sometimes, our people don't know what is best for them. That's why God made some men masters and some servants."

Amanda put her sewing down and reached for the Bible, thumbed up front in Genesis and read aloud, "In the sweat of thy face shalt thou eat bread, till thou return unto the ground, for out of it wast thou taken: for dust thou art, and unto dust shalt thou return."

Mrs. Milford nodded. "I married Mr. Milford, even though it meant coming here and getting used to an entirely new way of life. Slavery is an abomination."

So why did you sell Sally away? When you knew Virgil was coming with the money? But she kept silent. "I see."

"I pay all of my servants a fair wage. They will tell you how well I provided for each of them."

"I understand."

"But you don't agree."

Amanda rested the Bible on her knees and stared at the frowning older lady. "If everything was so wonderfully resolved, I wonder why I'm risking my husband's anger by spending time with you."

"That's your affair."

"Yes, it is. But something about his former enslavement has him captive. It's preventing him from being fully happy."

"I don't see why."

"I don't either. From what my father said, slavery also enslaved the masters. I wonder if you are as happy as you can be here, as you face God's judgment."

"Just a few years ago, I could have people who look like you whipped for saying less than that."

March noticed the distinctive change in the feel of the room and edged closer to Amanda. The little girl sat quiet and still at the base of the chair, facing the window.

"Like Sally? Did you have her whipped before you sold her to support yourself?"

"Sally?"

"You remember who she was?"

"Of course I do, but it's none of your affair." The old woman folded up her piecework. "Maybe there's been enough sewing today."

"I understand. I also understand that if you have burdens on your heart that are heavy, you should take them to God. He'll be there for you, always. That's what I've done lately so I could be of support to my new family. And I thank you for that new family."

"You're welcome." Mrs. Milford's curt voice came short as she sat up straighter.

"Still, I cannot help but think of how much better you would feel if you admitted the role you played in creating unnecessary pain in Virgil's life. I hope you will pray on it and come to a resolution of peace." Amanda stuck her needle in the edge of her own piecework and carefully rolled it up.

"I had him bring you down here, missy, and I can send you back too."

"You certainly could, ma'am. But you won't. You've already deprived him of one wife. I don't think you would do it again. It wouldn't be right."

Mrs. Milford shifted in her chair. "I guess they teach insolence to your betters up there at that college."

A hot feeling shot through Amanda. She took March by the hand. "I know not anything about my betters, ma'am. Only about how God has placed us here on this earth to get along and make our own special contributions in this life. Equally. I hope that you'll remember the lesson you seemed to have known so long ago before you came to Georgia. Good day to you, ma'am."

Mrs. Milford said nothing but nodded. At the last minute, March slipped from her handhold and ran back to Mrs. Milford and kissed her sunken-in old cheek.

"March," she called. Her daughter returned to her and slipped her hand inside of hers again. Taking strength from the feel of her little bony fingers, Amanda prayed about what she had said.

The shine of tears on Mrs. Milford's face was hard to forget.

Chapter Sixteen

Milledgeville and Milford were half a day apart. Virgil had started out late and knew better than to be on the roads past dark, but it was summertime and the light stayed a bit longer. What drove him and his horse, though, was the thought of Mandy waiting. His wife, Mandy Smithson.

Pie breathed hard when he pulled up at the house. The house was empty. Didn't she have Saturday school? But the schoolhouse was empty as well. Maybe she'd let them go early.

He switched horses and rode into Milford. He went to Pauline's first.

"How'd it go?" Pauline called from her doorway.

"Went fine. I put in my papers. So there's an election to come."

"And my Isaac will be able to vote."

He swallowed and climbed down from his horse. That was still up in the air. Negro men were talking about running for office, but strange enough, their right to vote was not secure. Not yet. "You see Mandy and March?"

"She had the Saturday school today. Came back here with me. Asked a lot of questions about Sally."

Why wasn't Pauline looking at him? His heart beat fast. Pauline was too direct. It wasn't like her not to look at him. She was always kind of making fun of him to his face. It was fine, since Pauline had a good soul. But now this. "You tell her."

"She had to know some things. Not all."

"What she say?" He pulled the horse to the pump to get a drink of water, feeling like he needed one too.

"Like it was all sadness. She trying so hard, Virgil. You got to give her some understanding."

"I do." He remembered the colorful dresses worn by the beautiful wives of Negroes hoping to run for office. His Mandy would outdo all of them.

"Then she wanted to go up to the big house."

He stopped. "What for?"

Pauline folded her arms and looked at him. "She from the north. She don't know that old woman like you and me. She think she can talk to her cause they both Northern people. Bless her heart, its like she being led into the fiery furnace."

Knowing what had happened to Meshach, Shadrach and Abednego, Virgil said a quick prayer for her. But he was so confused. After he'd told her not to go, not to have anything to do with Mrs. Milford…

She didn't listen. Of course.

"Maybe if you had a told her the story yourself, she wouldn't have to go looking for answers. She think she helping you to greatness."

"Digging up all that old mess don't help nobody."

"If she think you still love Sally, it does. Amanda's your wife before God and the law now. You better show her some love, afore she gets it into her head to get on the train and go on back to Ohio, just like you wanted her to afore."

"She ain't going to do that."

"You thinking it cause of March. Well, she love that little girl, powerful much, but she knows I cared for her afore. If she think she's in your way, she'll get out of it." Pauline poked the sleeve of the light broadcloth coat Mandy had made him so he'd be cool in the summer. "Just cause she say she ain't have nowhere to go doesn't make it so."

He patted the horse down, thinking about what Pauline had said. "Well, your Isaac have to be at the forge more if I got mayor business."

"No problem with me. He do better, I be better too. Have more time for learning. Then I can read the Bible myself, 'stead of listening to your hot air Bible stories all the time. See if what you telling us is right."

He gave a slight smile and shook his head.

In the distance, across the town square, the strains of a small song floated on the wind. March's voice. Virgil stepped forward, and a small figure dancing around a taller stately figure appeared.

"There they be." Pauline inclined her head toward them. "How you going to greet your wife? You going to act as if you like her or like she a burden? What you going to do?"

"Peace, Pauline. You had your say."

"I be saying more when I feel like it. You just never met someone who don't believe everything coming out of your mouth ain't a prayer book. 'Cept for me. Send March to me for a cookie. You need to talk to your wife."

Virgil guided the horse to a post and tied it up. He stepped into the town square as his daughter ran over to him. He scooped her up and gave her a kiss. "Pauline say she got a cookie for you. You allowed to have one afore we go on home."

Small cries of happiness came from March as she ran to Pauline's house.

Mandy came closer. Her silhouette without the wide skirt was smaller, but she still presented the picture of dignity.

"You coming from Mrs. Milford's."

She lifted her head and stared directly at him. The hazel glints presented in her eyes. "I did."

"After I told you not to be bothered."

"My father's name was Lawrence Stewart. Your name is Virgil Smithson. You are not my father."

"Different men, too."

"Are you referring to the fact that he had a college education and you don't? The difference there can be the work that you want to put into your studies instead of standing here upbraiding me because I went to visit a lonely old woman."

"To get information."

"To see if she is ready to face up to what she's done."

He couldn't help a bit of a smile. "You taking up preaching?"

"I teach. That's what I do. I wondered if she'd ever given a moment's thought to what she'd done. All her trying to be a benefactor, have you be mayor, and the rest. Was it enough to make up for what she did?"

Was it? It didn't matter to him. But it did matter. For Sally. "What she say?"

"She threw me out and told me to mind my own business."

"Sound like the first right thing that old woman say."

"I don't like the looks of her skin. She won't be here long. Maybe if she considers you as her minister."

He gave a laugh, like a hoot owl at night. "She like to hear me preaching. Rev. Arnold is her minister."

"He wouldn't forgive her. She needs forgiveness before she leaves this earth."

"Good thing she throw you out. 'Cause if she think she getting it from me, she fool crazy. Let's get on home. I'm hungry for dinner."

Instead of striding ahead of her as he might have before, he stood next to her and took her small hand into his. He walked toward Pauline's house with her, enjoying the feel of her brown plaid skirt swishing next to his pant leg. The feel of that skirt comforted him in a way he had not understood before. If he, as a preacher, had ever doubted his faith he knew different now. By providing him with this woman, he knew God was by his side.

Virgil's hand closed over hers in a comforting way. His hand was like a hug, and there were days when she needed that very much. She didn't know how, but she knew that she had done the right thing, visiting Mrs. Milford, but still had a feeling that she'd offended Virgil in some way. Asking him if he were angry with her made no sense, so she just relished the feeling of her hand in his and prayed. *Please, God, help me reach his heart.*

That was all she could do. She was just one simple woman. Asking God for anything else seemed to be asking for too much.

Pauline seemed to leap all over her when they reached her door. "What she say?"

Amanda made a funny face. "She told me to get out of her home. She may not invite me back ever again."

"You don't want to be up there anyway. That was Sally's bad place. No need for you to be up in there."

"I know what you all are saying, but she's just an old woman."

Pauline folded her arms and nodded. "For some people. For most of us, she's a reflection of bad old times."

March ran up to her, wrapped her little arms about Pauline's skirt, and squeezed. Pauline smiled down at her and ruffled up her braids. "Get on, you. We be at church tomorrow."

"Yeah. Better get on, but Mandy, you need to think on what I'm going to say. Wives need to obey their husbands."

"Virgil, I don't think—" Amanda started, but Virgil squeezed her hand and smiled.

Pauline waved a hand in the air. "You best stop funning with that girl, or you'll answer to me. Take her on home."

"You want up on Pie's back?" he asked his wife.

"I can walk. That's what me and March were doing anyway."

"I sure feel funny if you both were walking and I was the one riding."

Pauline shook her head. "We be here all day with you all and this courting behavior. Virgil, get upon that horse and you too, Mandy. March can walk. She got young legs."

Virgil did as he was told and reached his hand down to Amanda who jumped on, almost as if she were in his lap. "Go on 'head, March. We see you."

March ran off like the wind was after her, and they all laughed.

Pauline wiped her eyes with her apron corner. "You gave that child her dream. She want to run all over the place without anyone telling her what to do or to slow down."

"It's why her food doesn't stay by her, I guess."

"Yeah. Hard to keep it on her. Her mamma was the same way."

With their faces so close, Amanda tried to turn away a bit, to give him some space, but it didn't work well. He reached around her and gently slapped Pie's back. Their friend seemed to smile at their discomfort and waggled her fingers at them. "See you all in church."

Virgil grunted a little. "Fine, Pauline."

They rode on, watching March skip, jump, and fairly cartwheel up the hill to their home. It pleased Amanda to watch the child enjoy herself. Thank the dear God that there was no such thing as slavery to tame her spirit. Still, though, her spirit had to be tamed.

"How was the city?"

"Milledgeville is only a bite bigger than Crumpton. You wouldn't hardly know it for a city. The Yankees destroyed it something terrible. Only reason Milford farm escaped that treatment was cause Mrs. Milford was a Yankee before she married. Now she swear she die here."

"She may sooner rather than later." Amanda spoke right into his smooth shirt, one she had ironed herself.

"That woman will outlive us all."

"She looks slightly worse every time I see her. As Father did."

"Mandy." He spoke above her head, trying not to interact with her, it seemed. "I'm sorry, honey. I forget you been so strong and just doing what you had to do. I forget about your daddy. You must miss him."

Oh, yes. She did. Somehow, though, as she bounced on the back of this horse, jouncing just the slightest bit against Virgil's chest as the horse climbed up the hill, seemed to make everything a little easier to bear. "I've been reading his diaries. I'm doing as he would want me to do. I feel like a warm blanket is around me."

Was that the thing to say when a man's arms, made strong with the strokes of the blacksmith's hammer, surrounded her? Her dimples, the hateful things, probably sunk six inches deep in embarrassment. "I mean, I'm comforted by knowing that helping the enslaved is his work. He wanted me to help him in his work, but now, in carrying it on, I know I'm making him proud."

"I understand."

Regretfully, the horse was coming to the end of the path.

"Thank you." She didn't know what to say. How very strange to suddenly be cradled in this man's arms.

"I just want you to know. When you comes to Milledgeville—or wherever they going to put the capital—you going to do your father proud there as well."

"Thank you. I would hope so."

She slid off the horse which hitched her skirts up behind her. She turned quickly and adjusted them. March came running over to help. "No harm done, Mamma. Your slips are fine."

"Thank you, March. Let's make dinner while your father puts the horse up, shall we?"

"We shall." The child slipped her hand in Amanda's, and they went inside. How did one even begin to talk to a husband? She hoped she had made a start today, but it was so difficult to know if what she had done was right.

When so much of what she had done in his life was wrong.

"Mandy, you a beautiful lady, and it a lucky day when you became my wife."

The words were much easier to say to Pie than to Mandy. Pie seemed to agree much more with it too.

But Pie didn't have no dimples and no hazel glints. Nice horse, but he didn't even come close to Mandy.

Time come to pray.

Lord Almighty. I know you got to help me find the words for my sermon tomorrow. But there's some other words I got to say to Mandy, and I needs your help. She ain't like any woman I ever known, and it's hard to find a way into her heart and mind. Please help me find a way there. So's we can live together in peace.

Praying always helped him to feel better even as he waited for an answer. However, the answer came to him.

Let go of Sally.

"I let go of Sally." He spoke the words, but they didn't sound real in the air.

Let her rest in peace.

He knew what this meant. Everything he felt about Mrs. Milford crowded out the room he was supposed to have for Mandy. Did he have to go see Mrs. Milford to clear that space?

"Don't want to." He picked up the curry brush and started brushing down the horse. While he made the broad strokes, he understood what Mandy had tried to do. And she had done it by willfully disobeying him.

He put down the brush and led Pie out of her stall. "Just a little more, girl. I gots something to do."

March stood on the front porch. She musta been done helping her mother with dinner. He spoke to her. "Tell your mamma I'm going to be right back. She don't have to wait dinner for me, but I need to do something."

He rode at a good clip to the Milford house because he was hungry, to be sure, and because he wanted to get this over with.

Charles opened the door before Virgil finished climbing the front steps of the porch. "I need to see her," Virgil said.

"Your wife came in here today and upset her something awful. She don't need to see you."

"I'll be just a minute. You come on so I ain't in there alone."

Clearly, Charles didn't want to. He was one of the old timey ones who thought the end of the old times was the end of the world because it brought up brash Negroes like Virgil. Charles would do whatever he needed to protect Millicent Milford, so he came along.

"Virgil? Is that you?" she called. "Come from the capital?"

Mrs. Milford sat up in bed, her two pigtails sticking out. Yeah. She looked a sight. Maybe on the way to meet her Lord. Even as a preacher, he wasn't used to seeing that. He'd held Sally while all of her blood drained out of her thin body from that white baby she'd birthed, but Sally had been in the flower of her youth. Mrs. Milford's sunken features were something different.

"Come and pray with me, Virgil."

Yes. He needed to pray. He bowed his head. "Dear God, please come into the room today and help us know the power of your healing light and mercy, the power of your forgiveness. Help us make room in our hearts for the new. In your name, amen."

"Amen. You file the papers?"

"I did. Signed my own name too."

"That wife of yours taught you? She succeed where I couldn't, eh? Well, she's something, coming up in here like butter wouldn't melt in her mouth and asking me about Sally."

"Well, way I see it, ma'am, she right. She want to know about Sally. And I'm asking you for the first time, what did you buy with that money?"

"Virgil, it's all up in this house. Times got hard. I used that money to keep the place running. To patch the roof, to feed us, to keep living." She spread her hands. "There isn't any one thing. It was a foolish, desperate act on my part, but I had to keep going somehow."

"Not one thing?" He wanted that thing in his hand so he could smash it. What could he do to the house but burn it down over Mrs. Milford's head?

"I'm sorry. I wouldn't have done it, knowing what I could get for her. She was the most valuable one after you. I was going to make a crop and buy her back."

"There's no way to buy back slaves when you selling them into Alabama, Mrs. Milford."

"I'm from the north. I didn't know that."

"You do now." Virgil stood up. "Sorry for wasting your time."

"Yes, well. At least I know you filed the papers. As you should have. You will do a lot of good for this community. Amanda will too once she learns to mind her own affairs. You tell her now."

In the past, he would have said, "Yes, ma'am," and stepped out. Instead he said, "Goodnight, Mrs. Milford. Rest up."

"Don't know as I'll be in your church in the morning, but I appreciate you coming here to pray for me in my bed of affliction." He tried not to think about how her voice shook as he walked out of her bedroom. Was Amanda right about the woman's health?

Virgil strode out of the house, but instead of going back to Pie and home, he went to the slave cemetery next to the house. Milfords and slaves to the Milfords rested in side by side cemetery plots. Sally rested here. Her many brothers and sisters knew where she was because he'd made her a special marker of iron, one that would last a long time.

It just said, "Sally Smithson. Mother and wife."

The bad old times had done everything to pull them apart. He would always care for her and respect her because she was March's mother, but would she have looked like those freemen's wives, being on his arm in the capital building in Milledgeville? She didn't have Mandy's grace or manner about her. Sally had been shy and withdrawn.

Who was he to question God's plan? He was just a simple man trying to make things better for his people. Trying to bring light where it didn't exist. "Rest easy, Sally. We bringing up your child to be a proud woman."

When she and her baby had died in his arms, he'd brought her body back here to Georgia to rest in her home and put her mark of shame, the large baby boy who had ripped her apart, into her arms.

He did it to show he understood she couldn't resist or say no.

He did it to say he forgave her.

CHAPTER SEVENTEEN

Teaching had not been a career Amanda aspired to at Oberlin. She had thought to assist her father. Thank the Lord this opportunity had come up when her father's illness increased in intensity. The children in the school learned fast, and March's progress was especially pleasing. Whip-smart March took to her schooling with ease. Bless the children's hearts, they indulged her as the leader of the children. It may have been maybe because of her father, but March also had natural leadership capabilities.

What would March be in the future? A maid to Mrs. Milford? She got a little glimpse into Virgil's concerns for his daughter as she watched March play with the other children in front of the school. No. Teaching might be more suitable. Oh, well. March's special role as the daughter of her heart was an appropriate one then.

Never question the ways of the Lord.

During recess, Virgil sometimes came from the smithy to have lunch at the house. She always laid it out for him but never came home to eat with him since she watched the children play. She enjoyed sitting on the front steps and supervising the games, watching March take her natural step into leadership but still kind to all.

Today, she was surprised to see Isaac come instead on Virgil's horse.

"Boss man sent me to get his lunch. Busy day today, but he say how do to you and he be along home to see you later."

"That's fine. Tell him the same thing from me. Plates are on the front table."

Isaac rode toward the house.

After he'd disappeared, a group of men on horseback came down the road. Amanda thought nothing of it, but the children corralled into the schoolhouse, even though she'd not called an end to recess. The men pulled up at the water pump in front of the school. One of them was the storekeeper from Crumpton and she didn't quite remember his name. Odd. Didn't he have a store to run in the middle of the day? Why were they here?

"'Day, Mrs. Smithson," the storekeeper addressed her. "How do?"

She stood up, still marveling that every single one of her thirty students had filed into the schoolroom, taking their homemade ball with them. "Hello. May I help you?"

"Just on the road. Can we water our horses?"

"Surely." She spread out her arm in welcome. It wasn't in her to deny an animal water.

"Husband around?"

She hesitated in offering up this information. Maybe they genuinely needed to see Virgil on town business, but would it be wise to say anything about him not being in the near vicinity?

She opened her mouth, but felt the wind stir. Isaac had ridden up beside her, holding Virgil's lunch plate in one hand. "Boss man is down at the smithy. I take him any message you need as you riding through Milford here."

A chill went up her arms. Isaac's response to these gentleman sounded nothing like the type of response Virgil had coached her to give. It did not escape her notice, either, that the men were coming in a direction away from Crumpton.

"Just taking a look around. Nice little schoolhouse here."

"Thank you." Amanda spoke up. They didn't mean it as a complement, but, with God's help, she viewed as such.

A man in the back spoke. "We need a schoolhouse ourselves. White children should learn to read first."

His name occurred to her. "I've sent letters to my school in Ohio to see if anyone would want to come to your fine town and open a school. If the letters don't travel fast enough, I'll be happy to give Mr. Daley a telegraph, if there are means to send it."

The shopkeeper nodded. "Letters posted last week. Probably take some time to get one of them fancy schoolteachers down here like Mrs. Smithson."

His look at her resembled Charles Henry's glances too much.

"Can't have Negro teachers teaching white children."

She looked the man square in the face. "It might please you to know that the majority of my class was of your race. Only three of us Negroes graduated, and the other two gentlemen have jobs elsewhere. If you've watered your horses suitably, I'll continue with the school day and keep Mr. Daley posted on any developments regarding a teacher for your town. I bid you a good day."

Most of them didn't understand what she'd said, but Mr. Daley did. He was the one who mattered. Her heart beat rapidly and her breathing became shallow, although she didn't understand why. It wasn't as if she were afraid of these men, was it?

"Mrs. Smithson said good day. Think that's a fine idea," Isaac balanced Virgil's lunch with ease.

"You up there carrying lunch for your boss man, boy? I'm feeling hungry myself." Mr. Daley sneered, and they all laughed in a guttural, deep, mean-sounding way.

Amanda spoke up, praying this wouldn't turn into something ugly. "There aren't many places to eat along the highway as you travel. If you are in need of something, I have a stew I can share in Christian fellowship." Her mind went to the rabbit stew bubbling in the house for Virgil's dinner, but she would make him something else if a simple stew would keep these men in a hospitable frame of mind.

Instead of the leering, lewd look he fixed her with before, Mr. Daley stared at her as if she had two heads. "No. We're done here. I'll let you know of letters coming through. But mind—this school needs to stop meeting or we'll make it stop. Got my meaning, girl? "

"I believe I do." She smoothed down her skirt to show calmer than she felt. "Good day."

"Good day."

The men got on their horses and rode back toward Crumpton. *Thank God.*

The shuffle of little feet on the porch of the schoolhouse stirred her, and the children peered out. They'd had better sense than she'd had, certainly, to hide. Her heart hurt, thinking about how they knew so well what to do when four strange white men approached them. She certainly didn't.

"Virgil ain't going to like the way they was talking."

"Are you going to tell him?"

"'Course I am. Soon's as I take him his lunch. He needed to know about this."

She wished Virgil didn't have to be bothered. He had enough on his mind already. "Back inside, students. Time for our numbers."

Usually, the children would have groaned or tugged at her skirts in rebellion. Today, though, they all went inside and sat still at their desks, not saying a word. Every single youthful spirit, including March's, had been crushed into submission. The appearance of four men at their doorstep had done that to them.

How completely unfair. She took up her primer, prepared to give them the information they needed to lift their chins with pride and move forward in their lives.

"Did she have her gun in her hands?"

"Virgil, she was out there on the road a'talking to them. Didn't have no gun. It was just her. She offered them stew. And they didn't touch her. It was like the spirit of the Lord shone through her. They had no response for her. She was just as brave—"

"Didn't ask about bravery." He put down the shoe he was beating out, fear freezing his veins, far from hungry for the cold chop and sliced potatoes on the plate. It was easy enough to heat up food here in the fires, but he wouldn't have been able to eat it. The tools he held became harder to hold because of the slickness in his palms. What kind of fool was he to build the schoolhouse facing the main road rather than in the town?

Thought there'd be a male teacher coming.

Truth there. A man would have protected the schoolhouse. Now Mandy was alone, by herself, and not using her gun to protect herself as he told her to? He fairly couldn't work because of his worry.

Putting down his tongs, he shouted to a startled Isaac, "I'll be right back."

He grabbed his rifle and snatched off his leather apron, fear beating in his chest, making his middle ache at the thought of Mr. Daily returning to the school with his bunch of friends. He thought of what could happen to Mandy, a tiny, in that schoolhouse with those children by herself. She could end up like Sally. Anything happen to Mandy, and it'd mean he'd messed up again, abandoning a woman to the ways of the world.

Dear God, please protect Mandy and the children until I get there. Let them be okay until I can protect them. Please, help her to understand how this is a different world down here and she just can't go on the main road offering meals to strange men, even Mr. Daily. Help us, Lord, in your name. Amen.

Talking with God sealed it in his mind. If they were going to go to Milledgeville, they would go as a family. He could not, would not, leave his wife behind anymore.

He rode Pie up the hill as if her tail were on fire and didn't even stop to tie her up. The horse knew to stay in front of their house and the schoolhouse. Rifle in hand, he clambered up the stairs of the schoolhouse and kicked open the door, wood chips flying off and children screaming.

Mandy stood in front of the classroom, holding up her custom-sized rifle. The very rifle that accompanied her to school every day now. The rifle he had promised her before he left for Milledgeville, She pointed it. Or thereabouts.

Trust her to do exactly as he told her. At this moment.

She put it down upon seeing him and ran to him, skirts flying. "Virgil, what are you doing here?"

"Papa!" March exclaimed and danced over to her father. He gave her a brief hug. "Go sit down now. You in school."

March obeyed instantly.

"Yes, school is in session. We didn't expect you to come crashing in here."

Why was she all mad? "I had to see what was going on. I fix the door."

"See that you do. We were in the middle of a math lesson."

"Good to see you had your rifle on you, at least."

"Is that what this is about? Because when I was on the road, I didn't have it?"

"I told you how you needed protection on you all the time. You don't have that, then you might as well offer yourself up to them."

"Well, I didn't. I used reason and logic to speak to them."

He snorted. "A lot of good that would do if one of them got off his horse and treated you like his…"

He spoke into silence. The entire classroom's attention was riveted on their quarrel. Do God, this woman stirred up his blood faster than anyone he had ever known before! He quieted himself and turned from her.

"I get the tools to fix the door before I go back to the smithy."

"See that you do. We need it for protection."

He stomped out, his boots echoing across the schoolhouse porch. Why did she have to be right, in the middle of all of her fancy talking? He guided Pie to a post, went to the house to get the tools, and came back to fix the door, listening to Mandy leading the children in a song about God, one of his favorites. "Do Lord, oh do Lord, oh do remember me…."

By the time he was done with the door, some of the parents had gathered to pick up their children from school. Didn't see the need to tell them about the visitors from the road. He told them he'd messed up the door. Many snickered as they left. Glad he could be some entertainment, just for them.

March spun and danced up to the house, leaving Mandy in the schoolroom with him. He packed up his tools and stood there, looking at the door. It was a job well done, but he had wasted time at the smithy. Good thing Isaac's training was in a good place so he didn't have to fall too far behind down there.

Still, she stood behind him with her arms folded. She wore the blue-stripey wedding dress. Made her look chipper, usually, except for now since she didn't look that happy with him. "The door looks very nice. Thank you."

"You welcome." He started to walk away, then stopped. "I'm sorry. I didn't act right."

Mandy sighed. "You acted out of emotion. I'm not entirely sure what emotion, but that's not always a problem."

"Emotion?"

"Yes. Did you think those men were attacking me? As Sally had been?"

"Maybe I did."

Mandy laid a hand on his arm. "I'm not Sally."

"That's for true. I mean, you're very different."

"And since we are different, then you don't need to worry in the same way."

"Don't know. You still learning about how it is down here."

"And I am. With your guidance and help."

He put his hand on top of hers and squeezed it. "Just have to make sure, is all. Man can get lonely around here sometimes."

"And have to cook his own dinner?"

"That's it. And no grape pies."

She pulled her hand from under his, put it on top, and squeezed her thumb there. A strange feeling spread through his fingers, and he couldn't help but wonder how new this all was to her. Surely someone as beautiful as her had had some male attentions before him.

"Well, I'll be sure to make what you like. But you have to know to trust me sometimes."

He pulled his hand out, just for a second, and set it on her shoulder. "I didn't know your daddy. But I get the sense from what I know about him from you that he didn't want you to be all alone in the world. You told me about his partner, tried to have his way with you. Isn't that right?"

He didn't mean to make her sad, afore God, but the dimples went away. He pulled her into the circle of his arms and held her, and, to his surprise, she stayed there. Her fingers splayed against his chest, and he felt her smooth touch through the cloth of his shirt. Cloth might protect people in some cases, but it wasn't protecting him from the weird squiggles of—what she call—emotion, from him feeling.

Oh, God. Help me.

'Cause that feeling was dangerous. It made him let his guard down, and that wasn't good for him or her or March. He would protect her all the time. He'd promised.

But, with the way she felt in his arms, and the orange smell coming from her smooth, flat braids, he understood now.

God would have to protect him.

The cloth of his shirt slowly dampened. He pulled her from him. White, salty tear tracks traced their way down her brown features. "Don't cry, Mandy. Please."

"I'm just—I thought of Papa. What you said was right. I throw myself forward when I shouldn't, and maybe I shouldn't have this time. It came out all right with those men, but I never even thought of what might happen if they carried me off..."

"Well, they didn't. Isaac was up getting the lunch, and it all worked out to the good."

"Thank you for caring about me."

With his thumb, he wiped away the accumulating salt in her dimple. There should not be any tears in those dimples. Her dimples stood for happiness and good times.

He wiped again and intended to pull back, but before he knew it, she reached up and pulled him close, down to her pink lips, pulling him into that sweet abyss of her kiss.

Help me.

There was no help for him from this scamp of a Northern woman. He knew it from the moment he'd laid eyes on her on that train platform. She fit under the crook of his arm for a purpose and in his arms perfectly. For this purpose.

She traced her fingertips on the back of his neck as she pulled him deeper into her kiss. A different kind of sound came forth from Mandy. A little teeny sound, but it was a sound that told him to get himself together. A groan. *Do God.*

Stop kissing on this woman in full view of the road. No way for a preacher to act.

But she was his wife before God. And the courthouse. All legal and everything. No one, not even those men, could take that away from them.

He pressed his hand on her shoulder and eased her sweet pink lips from his. "Mandy, we don't know who's coming down the road."

"Do we care?" The dimples came on back.

His heart lightened at the sight, but still… "We care. There's a time and a place, Mandy. You understand?"

"And under earth a season to its purpose." That scamp quoted the Bible. To him. "Maybe you'll take me someplace and teach me a different lesson."

"Mandy!" he breathed out. His heart beat fast.

"Take up your tools, Virgil. I know you must have more work down at the smithy. Thank you for helping."

She gathered her books and walked up the rise to the hill, greeting their daughter on the front porch of the house.

Satisfied she was in a safe place, he climbed on Pie's back and guided the horse back to the smithy. Had Mandy said what he thought she'd said, that she wanted to be his wife in heavenly fullness, as God would have them be?

Do God. He wanted that too.

He had to make sure she wanted it. He would not chase her away by acting out of turn or by upsetting her with improper advances. Certainty was crucial here.

He had to care for her feelings. Those had to be protected as well.

Instead of feeling fear for the coming night, he whistled as he guided Pie into the stall of the smithy, ready to get back to work on someone else's horse.

CHAPTER EIGHTEEN

When the previous month began, all she wanted was to escape the vile clutches of Charles Henry. Now she lived a new life, and part of it involved a man who seemed to care for her. Oh, those Oberlin days of rebuffing the attentions of her male school chums seemed so far away and long ago. So much of this life in the South was what her father had sought to protect her from, but the end of slavery had brought her to a purpose—a purpose to give her life meaning that her father would be proud of. And Virgil.

She dished up the stew and waited for him to return from the smithy. When he did, Virgil bristled coming through the door, a quite different state than when they last parted.

"I was made the mayor of one town, not two."

"What do you mean?" She came to him, not shy about standing next to him. She handed him a cake of sweet soap and a warmed kettle of water for his pre-dinner wash.

"Those men from Crumpton, without Daily, came down to the smithy on their way to see Mrs. Milford. They expecting me to shut down the school until their teacher comes."

Despite the kettle of hot water between them, a chill went up her arms. "Why would that be?"

"A whole lot of foolishness of having the Negro children get ahead of the white ones."

"That is foolishness." Her students were bright, eager, and capable, but they had years of limited or no exposure to their letters and numbers. They had a lot of catching up to do. "Would those people be so firmly fixed in not having the races learn together down here? That's how I went to school at Oberlin."

Virgil stripped down to his bare chest and used the warm water and washrag to soap himself up. He had a sprinkling of black chest hair where the muscles were the most prominent and hardest.

Amanda wanted to avert her eyes.

She couldn't.

He was truly a breathtaking sight to behold. Another one of God's creations. The same as looking at a deer in the woods.

Except looking at deer didn't make her skin tingle all over or her hands grow clammy with sweat.

"They ask me to do something about it as mayor and as your husband."

The prickles disappeared. "Do what?"

"Shut down the school."

"That's not going to happen."

"I knew you say that." He dried himself with the towel and reached for the fresh shirt she held out, eyes averted a bit. Everything on him rippled like water on a pond. Was the hair soft or crisp? No need to think of it now. He buttoned up his shirt and tucked the ends into his pants.

"What should I say?" she asked.

He seemed surprised by her response. "You about teaching the children—and the adults sometimes. You do what you have to do. I'm the mayor. I'll do what I have to do to figure this out. I never even thought they cared about no school."

She shook her head. "It's not the school. It's what it stands for. It means an end to what was. People are always resistant to change."

"Still, you need to keep your rifle handy. I'ma eat dinner and go make a rack for your gun at the school. Should have made one anyway."

There went her special meal. Virgil barely noticed the savory rabbit stew. His concern marked his face and the rigid set of his large hands. She and March cleaned up the dishes and sat down to their sewing work. It was only when March had to go to bed that he came back in.

"Time for your lesson now." She approached him, after she had kissed March's sweaty little forehead good night.

"Not feeling it tonight, Mandy. I don't know why, I just don't like the feel of this. Maybe you should stop the school for a few weeks. Call it a picking vacation. Crops about to come in, and the children will be needed for that."

She shivered. "I can't do that. Making children pick up the crops. That's the same as…"

"We know." His intense gaze bore into her. "And if the children can still go to school it's like the old time all over again. Still, I just can't think of what else to do to get these people over the mad."

"I offered to send a telegraph. Mr. Daily said not to."

"Hmm. Yes. You need to go on to bed and get your rest."

"What about you?"

"I just feel a need to watch out for things. I'll be fine down here. Good night."

He took her hand and squeezed it, then let it drop, hands on his rifle again.

She wandered upstairs to begin the extensive ritual of brushing, rebraiding, and wrapping her braids to keep them flat as she slept. She tied her bonnet on and lay down to sleep, trying not to feel crushed under the weight of disappointment. The heat of the night was oppressive. Maybe this wasn't the best night to become Mrs. Smithson in the flesh.

She dreamed of a closed wooden gate. She kept lifting her legs on top of the posts but Virgil pushed her off to keep her on the other side. Charles Henry came along and grabbed her from behind, in all the wrong places, trying to push her over onto the wrong side. All the wrong dreams to have as Mrs. Smithson.

It wasn't in him to lie, especially not to Mandy. He had to bend the truth a bit because of that schoolhouse. The more he thought on it, the more he wished he could smack himself for his foolishness on where it was built. On top of it, two fools who called themselves night riders had taken it upon themselves to come to his smithy and disturb his peace while he was working. Even wanted their horses soled as they waited. He serviced them, but them showing up made the tools slip up in his hand—dangerous stuff for a blacksmith.

No. He couldn't face the prospect of Mandy, up there in her room, waiting for him in her nightgown as a wife should wait for her husband.

What if she was disappointed? What if she didn't love him the way he loved her?

Loved her. He did, and that's why he was sitting here on this porch. To protect her school.

What did he do to get her to understand that it was all for her protection? Get that stubborn woman to see it was best to let school out for a bit?

Could he work up the courage to do what he must? He couldn't believe that he was willing to do it after all the hours of work, all the hours of pain and frustration that he'd put into that schoolhouse.

If he were going to do it, everything would have to go, everything. He couldn't take the slates out. It all had to go. In a blaze of glory.

Please God. Forgive me for what I am about to do.

He put the gun in the rack at the house and got the kerosene out of the storage bin in the barn. Only needed a little bit and didn't want to waste it. It was better to let it go in a slow burn anyway. Sometimes, to clear land, he would start a little fire to have it go the way it needed to. He didn't want the fire to catch his house or the teacher house—those things should remain standing.

Only the schoolhouse should burn.

He poured the kerosene over the cracks of the floor. With a lit stick he had retrieved from the constant burning fire in the cookstove, he touched the corner of the schoolhouse closest to the door. Satisfied the burn would be steady, he closed the door on his handiwork and went home.

God promised Noah, no more water, but the fire next time. He put the kerosene back.

It was up to him to fix his mistake and do what he had to do to protect Mandy.

He could only pray that she understood.

Virgil climbed the stairs, one at a time, his feet aching. At the top stood a slice of white in the hallway. Standing there, trembling.

"What you doing up, Mandy?"

"I couldn't sleep."

He turned to face her. In the darkness, he couldn't be sure, but the faint glint of tears shone on her cheeks. Every time Mandy cried, it was 'cause of him. How would she be when she found out about the schoolhouse? Found out he was willing to destroy the heart of her work, of who she was, of who her daddy was? How could he even think of taking advantage of her in this way, on this night?

"I was worried about you." Mandy stepped closer, across the top of the stairs. She stood before him, visibly shaking in her white nightgown like an autumn leaf about to fall off the tree.

He only meant to stop her shaking. But he shouldn't have touched her on the shoulder. Warmth, like a healing balm, moved through his fingertips, into his hand, and up his arm, crossing into his body. He jerked his arm away, lest he be burned by her fire.

"No need. I'm fine." He quickly turned away to go back to his room, needing to leave her in the hall before he took her into his arms and did the base things he wanted to do.

But then she touched him. Her small hand rested on his arm and stopped him before he could walk off. Her hand and her body were small but still powerful enough to stop him in his tracks.

So he stayed.

And was consumed.

He pulled her into his arms and kissed her pretty lips, her neck, and shoulders. The fog clouded his mind, and he knew what it was to stand at the edge of Satan's fire.

Prayers came from his mind and his heart while loving her. His hands roamed all over Mandy and her white nightgown, in full appreciation of how God had fashioned her. Just for him.

Stop me, Mandy. Stop me.

She didn't. She wouldn't, and anger surged in his heart. Why didn't she stop him from doing this?

The devil thought came to him. *Because she's your wife. Legal. Recorded at the courthouse, legal wife. Nothing wrong with what you want.*

Still, as a preacher, he should be better than this. He should do better than this.

In that moment, he knew he was just a plain preacher man who could fall down. A human. When he took her by the hand and led her to the big pine bed, he knew he was human. Still he had carved that bed in the hopes that one day the right woman would be there to share it with him.

In the morning, he would need forgiveness from God. From Mandy, too. First, he had a promise to fulfill, and if she wanted to leave him after, he would completely understand.

He did not deserve her goodness.

But he meant to keep his promise.

In the morning, he did not look at her, almost as if he were ashamed. He dressed hurriedly and went to the schoolhouse, an odd move, even as she made breakfast.

Why was he concerned about the schoolhouse?

When she'd finished frying the bacon, she took the pans off the stove, told March to remain still, if possible, and went to the schoolhouse. In the open door, she stood and watched him squat in front of the fireplace. Stepping inside, she was hit by the strong odor. The schoolroom reeked of kerosene, and she wished she had a hanky to cover her face. She used her hand instead. "What happened here?"

Virgil stood and came to her, grabbing her by the shoulders. "What you doing here?"

"I wondered why you were over here rather than eating breakfast and making your way to the smithy."

"I be there soon."

"Why does it smell so? Someone tried to burn it?"

The horrifying thought came into her mind. The Crumpton night riders came here, trying to make sure that there was no school, trying to make sure the Negro children had no more school. Tears stood in her eyes. *Dear God*. What if the children had been in here? What if there had been a conflagration that set it all ablaze? *Thank you, God*. That was the proper response—praise that no life had been taken.

"The night riders came back to do it." She stepped away from the threshold, but as she did, the chill washed over her body. Why was Virgil here?

"No, Mandy. Not the night riders." He swallowed, and for the first time, a look of shame appeared on his face, a completely unfamiliar look that did not suit him. "Me. I did."

"You? You were going to burn the school?"

"Yes. Guess my burning didn't work, but can't have the children in here breathing this. Got to finish the job."

She couldn't breathe. "How could you?"

"How else could I stop you from having the school? I put this school in the wrong place. It's my fault, my work, so I got to fix it. By the time I build something new where I can protect you better, there be a teacher for Crumpton and the Milford school will have a chance."

"How?" Her breathing kept to a better pace, but it was still hard to speak. After everything, after last night, he would come next door and burn up her father's work, her work, what the school meant to the community.

She was married to this man. She didn't matter.

Staggering down the steps, she moved swiftly to the side of the steps and her stomach heaved up a small amount of bacon and biscuit into the red dirt. Virgil surrounded her with his arms, the same arms that held her so firmly in the night when she was soothed and persuaded that she was finally Mrs. Smithson. He guided her to the water pump to rinse her hands, face, and mouth. The cold water sluiced over her, bringing her back to reality.

Unfortunately.

"We can get March to pass the word around about no school today. You need to get in the house and lay down. Didn't mean for you to get sick. Must have been the kerosene." His grip, firm on her shoulders, reminded her that she was in a vise. This marriage held them together like a vise grip. He really didn't want it. He just wanted someone to take care of March and to clean and to…

Memories of last night's encounter in the hallway flooded to her. Shame washed over her like an ocean wave. Maybe she really was a soiled dove. Virgil was her husband, but then it hit her like an ocean wave, practically knocking her down. *Dear God.* He didn't even want her. It was all a ruse.

She really did have nowhere to go. The reality came sharp and strong, as pungent as the breakfast she'd thrown up. She wrenched away from him and went to her bedroom. Could she stay here and live with a man who would so easily set fire to her dreams, her work, and her father's work? Did she even know who he was?

Her head and mind spun, not unlike how she felt when Mrs. Milford made her suggestion to marry Virgil. She couldn't stay here. This was all a mistake. And a punishment for forcing God's will? She had forced his hand by coming down here, forced it by marrying this man and going into Crumpton and strutting around with her education, making the Crumpton folk want something they didn't have.

What was she doing there letting Charles Henry take over her father's responsibilities? No matter how he looked at her. She was doing Lawrence Stewart's work for sure, but he had also taken such loving care of her. There was justice to be done there as well. She had to see what had happened. Charles Henry needed to be questioned. In person.

She would go and make it right. The living was all she had in the world, and she needed to fight for it. There was nothing more for her here.

She pulled her valise out, folded two dresses into it, and gathered her comb and brush and pushed them in the valise too. She marched into the room where they had behaved so wantonly just hours before and saw her father's Bible on Virgil's night table. Scooping it up, she held the book like a shield against harm and walked down the stairs in a daze.

Virgil stood in the doorway of the dining area. "Mandy, what you doing?"

"Is March telling people there's no school?"

"She is. Some of the folk probably go on horseback to tell others. I was telling some folks too. Why you got your bag with you?"

She swallowed and stood as straight as she could. "Giving you what you want. I'm going."

"Put that bag down, Mandy. We're married in the sight of the law and the sight of God. You can't go nowhere."

"I can and I will. There are ways to end a marriage. Papa was an attorney, you know." Maybe he knew and maybe he didn't. Was an annulment out of the question now? It would be hard, but it could be done. Because she didn't know who he was anymore. If she ever did.

"Mandy, you sick, and kerosene clouded your head."

"No, the kerosene cleared my head. I'll be fine. But I'll need some of my salary for a train ticket."

Silence settled between them again. Like he'd done before, he let her make the decision. Again.

He let her arm go. "I'll take you down."

"I can walk."

"I'll ride you. Don't want March seeing you go. Likely tear her up."

"Don't bring March into this. You were about to burn up her school, the thing that you promised to Sally, that she would read and write. You might be a preacher, but you don't keep your promises."

"I do keep my promises. I made a promise afore God to protect you, but if you don't believe in that, ain't nothing I can do to tell you otherwise. I'll get the wagon ready."

"Fine."

She gave the house one look over. Such solid construction at Virgil's hand. It could look mighty fine, but not with her touch. The thought of some other woman making it prettier when she hadn't had the chance made her want to be sick all over again, so she went outside, just as Virgil pulled up with Pie and the wagon. He helped her up, and the same jolt went between them. She tried to pay no attention to it.

They said nothing to one another as he drove down to the platform. He waited as she waited.

Before she knew it, the train sounded in the distance. It arrived as Virgil pulled the wagon in front of the station.

She shouted, "Find March and tell her I love her. I miss her already."

"You her mamma. You tell her yourself."

"You're her father. Be that."

"Be her mamma. Come back home right now."

"You can direct everyone in this town just by your say so, but not me."

"We mean so little to you, you can leave us?"

"It's my life. I can do as I see fit."

He put a gold piece in her hand. Her pay. "You going back to Charles Henry?"

"You treated me like he wanted to." The gold piece sure didn't help.

Amanda stepped down on her own and spoke to the conductor. "The ladies' car, please."

His conductor's cap glinted a bit in the sun as he pointed it out to her, a little shocked at her request, but he didn't deny her. She might not get far in the ladies' car, but she would ride as a lady for as long as she could.

She turned on her heel and walked away from Virgil Smithson, determined to reclaim some piece, some portion of herself from him before he took it all, as if she were grape pie.

When she sat in the ladies' car and looked out onto the platform, she really wasn't surprised to see that Virgil wasn't there anymore.

She bowed her head. *Watch over the town of Milford, dear God. Bless them.*

It was all she had by way of a benediction.

The lurching in her stomach wasn't just the train. In leaving she'd abandoned her father's work. She would find some other way to make it good again in Ohio.

Hot tears slid down her face. She hadn't known it was possible to hurt more, but it was. She was cut in two again, as she'd been when her father died.

The train pulled away, and the last she saw of Milford was March in her papa's arms, crying as hard as she could.

In a moment, so was Amanda.

Chapter Nineteen

When March calmed down some, he left her at Pauline's house and drove up the hill in the wagon. If he were going to do this thing, he had to do it right.

No one would stop him. Mandy had left.

He took a lit stick from the smithy and stored the fire in an iron lantern on the corner of the porch. This time he could retrieve the slates and the few books.

Once the schoolhouse was emptied of all of the things he could move, he touched the lit stick to the porch and stood back to see what would happen.

Those pine boards needed better treatment when he built it again, for sure. This time fire caught too quick, too quick. The smoke arose faster than he would have liked. Well, in a terrible way, this burning taught him some lessons he would keep in mind in building the new schoolhouse. He would fashion it of brick, as he had his house, and build both church building and schoolhouse in the town square that way.

Only, why hadn't the fire caught the first time he had done it? What was God telling him? Maybe it was to send Mandy away, for her not to be his wife anymore. The knowledge felt like a heavy weight on his shoulders, dragging him low, nowhere near as high as he'd felt when he'd had Mandy on his arm, her dimples flashing, her skirt swishing by him. He could sign his own name to a document. He could read some of the Bible, picking more of the complicated words out each day. He knew more, and understood more than he had when she first came almost two months ago.

Holding the thin, shivering, shaking body of his distressed daughter, he understood how she felt and wanted to let loose in the same way. But he wasn't a child.

He would make the next building better and build it for God. Putting the schoolhouse and church next to his house had made him small and selfish. Putting it in the town square would make the building more for God's glory.

I'ma be better, next time. I promise.

The words carried him back to where he'd stood underneath Mrs. Milford's tree and promised to protect and care for Amanda. What was he doing here, cowering like a fool, letting her go? He was more worried about himself and his feelings than Amanda out there all alone. Was she going back to Ohio? To take up Charles Henry's idea?

No. She wouldn't do that.

Maybe she would go back to her school to get teachers. He thought of how she'd cut apart her own clothing to make a dress for his child, a child she had just met and didn't even know. That's how good she was, a good and faithful Christian woman God had gifted him. And he'd disappointed her.

The fire rose higher, taunting him, beckoning to him as he sat back and watched it burn. What had he done to his marriage to Mandy? He wanted to cover his face in his hands.

Except that bells rang out. The anvil from the smithy. The earth shifted as people began moving to the fire.

Do God. The whole town had left the fields and were coming to save the school. He had not told them what he was going to do.

The first ones up the hill were Pauline and Isaac, many others behind them. They panicked, seeing him sitting there, surrounded by books, slates and pencils. "What's going on?" Pauline cried out. "Who set fire to our school?"

"It was them men." Isaac stomped around, ready to form a posse headed for Crumpton. "They said they was going to do it. And they did it."

"Praise God the babies and Miss Mandy wasn't in the house," someone cried out. "Praise Him!"

"That true." Pauline turned to where Virgil still sat on the grass. "Pump water. We got to save the building."

The line began to form beside the pump. Virgil stood up when he saw their buckets. "Let it burn."

"What? Man, has you lost your mind? Where is Miss Mandy?" Isaac asked him.

"She not in that schoolhouse, is she?" Pauline shook him. "Dear God!"

"She's not in the schoolhouse!" He used his preacher voice, and people were still. "She gone. She left. I burned up the school-house. That's why all this stuff is out here on the road, so some of you start carrying it over to my barn for the new schoolhouse."

Pauline approached him with a timid look on her face, a look he was not used to seeing on her. "Virgil, are you right in your mind?"

"I'm fine. I made a mistake. I'm fixing it."

"Where's March?"

"She's down in your house. Left her there like I used to while I took care of this business up here. I didn't want her to see me burning down her schoolhouse."

"Why you burn it down?" Isaac asked. His face was moist, and not from sweat. "That schoolhouse meant something to more people than March."

Virgil could tell Isaac meant himself. "I know. But you saw them riders. You know Mandy. She wasn't going to stop having that school, no matter what we say. Them riders would have come back, waited until we was at the smithy, and they wouldn't care who was in the school." Virgil held up his hands. "We going to build it with brick in the town square and make it bigger and better. It's going to be fine. Let's pray."

They all fell to their knees. Usually he stood on these public occasions of prayer, but he fell to his knees like everyone else. "God," he shouted, "we need you today. We need your blessings to build up this school better and stronger in your name."

Usually someone started crying out, but this time it was more than one person. The group of distraught people held on to each other. The air was full of the sounds of sniffling. Quiet wiping on sleeves and handkerchiefs continued.

"It going to be all right," Pauline said, but she didn't sound as sure as she usually did.

"Anyone burn down our schoolhouse, it going to be us." Isaac sniffled.

Virgil laid a hand on his shoulder. "That's right."

"Where's our Miss Mandy? Why ain't she here?" someone shouted.

"Miss Mandy went on ahead to see about teachers for Crumpton so we can live side by side in peace."

Pauline's head popped up from the prayer. Hers wasn't the only one. "Hold on. You sent Mandy out into the world looking for teachers?"

Virgil's preacher voice abandoned him. "It's getting to be cotton chopping time, and the children are needed in the field."

God, tell Mandy to come back home.

"I allow that." Isaac said. "But why now? Why today?"

"We don't want to question folk about business. It was time."

"Naw." Pauline stood and temporarily towered over him. "You said something to that girl to make her go. Did you, Virgil? Say it out."

He stood too. "I said nothing. She was distressed about this whole business of the schoolhouse and them riders coming back. She thought it best to go on and find another teacher right now."

"You need to go on and get us our teacher back, lest she don't want to see hide nor hair of you."

"Why would that be?"

"I don't know, Virgil. Maybe you offended her somehow." Pauline stared him down.

The crowd grew silent. All that could be heard were the dying crackles of the burning schoolhouse. The smell of scorch lingered in the air.

"She my wife. How would I offend her?"

Someone coughed, probably to get a cinder cleared out from her throat.

Isaac shook his head. "Ain't for us to say, boss man. But you the one in charge. Seem like you need to get ready to get on the morning train."

He had given her his last money. He would have to go into Crumpton to trade for cash money, and they may not even have any. "Got to have money for a ticket. No need in wasting the town's money. She'll be back directly."

"We going to make sure of that." Pauline waved her arms. "What anyone got?"

Folks got mighty quiet. No surprises there. Cash money was hard to come by.

"Mrs. Milford will give us the money," someone said.

Pauline held up her hands and spoke, sounding like a preacher herself. "No. Ain't asking her for nothing. This is our town. Bad enough she got her name stamped all over everything. We going to get this ticket because, whether some likes it or not, Miss Mandy belongs here, not out there." She took off her field handkerchief and held it out. "I got five cents. Come on. Even if it's a penny. We going to send the mayor to get Miss Mandy and get her to come back to us."

Pauline went around the group. Some pulled out coins from pockets, chests, and other places. Some continued to pray. She stepped up to Virgil and handed him the money from the hanky. It would be enough to get him to Ohio, but beyond that he would have to sell something to bring them back. He would do as he must and stretch this blessing as far as it could go. "Thank you all."

"I got March. She stay with us. And she be fine because she know her mamma is coming back, right?"

Every single eye of the community stared at him. Never before had his political office come to be so meaningful. He was traveling on the trust of the town.

He put preacher strength into his voice. "Of course."

"She's going to be so happy, she ain't leaving no time soon, right?" Pauline said loud enough for all to hear.

Some in the back of the crowd snickered. Laughter? At their mayor? "Of course," he said.

"Just some honeymooning running off, I'll bet." Someone shouted out. More people laughed at him.

"Everyone go back to their mamma's house at least one time!" Calla Baxter said.

The laughter ramped up again, but Virgil shook his head. "Mandy don't have a mamma. She died awhile back."

Folks stopped laughing and got real quiet.

"She got that school," Isaac said. "That's where she going."

Oberlin. Her school. Her mother. And father. Would she be fool enough to visit Charles Henry? Could he convince her to come back? Would he make it in time to save her?

Amanda swallowed hard, chasing down the big lump in her throat. She stood on the street in front of Charles Henry's office. Her father's former office. A place where she would spend long Saturdays, reading, playing, and staring at the gilt-edged green wallpaper more days than she cared to count.

She had never thought she'd be back. But she'd known her father's former partner for a false man when she left, and the entries in her father's books drove her to ask more questions about how he could afford such a high living for her. He must have saved. If she could get a living here, then…

Then what? She could live on her own in the teacher's house. Just because she was married to Virgil didn't mean she had to live with him. They had fulfilled the requirements of the Christian community of Milford. She would live in the teacher's house and take care of March. Like a hired girl of sorts.

Except it might all be gone by now. Shudders went up and down her arms. How could Virgil have done it? Destroy everything he had worked so hard to build? She supposed he had the right, but still, the school had become so much more. He had to see that.

She took a handful of her black dress in hand. She'd been careful to come in mourning so Charles Henry would see her as her father's daughter and not as some Jezebel.

The new secretary made her wait. All day. Finally he said that Charles Henry was in court and did not intend to return until the morning, most likely. "You'll have to come back tomorrow," the man told her.

She did not bother to tell him who she was. Clearly, he thought that she was just some black woman and not the daughter of Charles Henry's former law partner. On her way to the boarding house she went by Oberlin to speak with some of her classmates. There she found success. Some promised her to teach a short summer session before the harvest time. For the adventure of it.

Early the next morning she returned to Henry's office. Still he'd beaten her there, and she had to wait extra long to see him. Fine, she had no other appointments.

When his day was over, she swept into his office in her smaller dress.

"Fine seeing you, Amanda," he said. "You look prosperous."

"Did you take my father's money into your keeping?" She had no time for small talk. "I would like the truth. If you have my living, I should want it for my own."

Charles Henry turned five shades of red. "I don't think it's very appropriate of you to come sweeping in here, wanting money of me."

"I want my father's money. There's a difference." She opened her reticule and pulled out a small thin book. "According to this portion of his diary, you owe him money. Something like nine hundred dollars, which seems small to you, I'm sure, but it means a great deal to an impoverished woman such as myself."

"Let me see that."

She was reluctant to hand it to him. But he wouldn't be able to escape her. She handed it over, her hand trembling.

As he examined the book, his look changed from one of worry to one of triumph, which made her stomach do flip-flops.

"Yes, these accounts were opened many years ago. To see to your mother's freedom. Your father owned me money many years to pay off her freedom. Of course, he was paying for two slaves, and not just one."

"My father would not have held slaves. That was against everything he stood for."

"Oh yes, he would have. Buying your mother was the only way that her former slave masters would let her go. He had to come up with a great deal of money quickly to ensure that they wouldn't come for her. Nine hundred dollars. Quite a sum back then, but then Aurelia was a top-notch ladies maid. Her mistress had been most distressed that she ran away. She had to be paid."

"I see. And the other?"

"Why, my dear. I thought you would have figured that out by now with your fine Oberlin education. That would be you."

"Me?" Her head lightened and filled with fuzz.

"You never wondered why your father was so protective? Why he sought to educate you? When you were born, your mother was a slave, and by Georgia law that made you one as well. The owners didn't care about a small baby, but of course you would increase in value as you grew."

"Increase in value?" Her repetition sounded foolish, but she could little help it.

"Yes. When he died, he had been paying me back for freeing you. So, my dear, it is you who owes me money, literally. I took into account what he had left when he died, but I was doing you a kindness, writing the rest off without claiming his books and such. The Milfords had been given full payment on you when you where about… six. The same age when they might have come for you to train you."

"Dear God." She held her chest to somehow contain her beating heart. It had to stay inside of her.

"Yes. Aurelia had free papers, but you didn't. They had not known about you, but if they had, they surely would have come for you as property. So he preemptively paid them so they wouldn't take you. When he died, he owed me about nine hundred dollars."

"And you said nothing when I came."

"I had other ledgers to show you. You left so fast. I had ideas, and you did not seem open to them. Then."

"Nor am I now. I'm married."

"I see your interesting wedding band. Your husband must not have nine hundred dollars. That is what I'm owed. For you."

Yes, that Tabulation class would have been most valuable. Now she understood how she read the numbers wrong. A pang for Virgil went through her. She was illiterate too in a way and that made her vulnerable. Except it didn't.

She stood up, no longer lightheaded. "We'll see to it that you get every penny."

"Who is he?"

"My husband is the town mayor and blacksmith in Milford, Georgia. I didn't not realize my connection to that place when I went south."

"Your father kept connection with them to follow the only family you have--your mother's siblings. I believe she had near twenty brothers and sisters."

She sat back down. Could she be related somehow to Isaac and Sally?

"Sounding familiar?"

Her head whirled. So much of the material of her father's estate had been sold off by her as the lone heiress to get to Milford in the first place. "I'll see that you are paid every penny."

"My secretary will make all of the necessary arrangements for the proper promissory note. Your father's determination about abolition takes on a whole new meaning, doesn't it? Good day, Amanda."

"My name, Mr. Henry, is Mrs. Virgil Smithson."

Charles Henry waved a hand. "Have him make it out however you like."

She stood on shaky knees. How would she make it back to the boarding house with this new knowledge? She went to the door and opened it, ready to sweep out as she had when she came in, except tension made the contents of her stomach roil.

Please let me hold on to my breakfast.

The outer door opened, and there, filling every corner of the door, stood Virgil Smithson.

He came instantly to her side. "You feeling fine, Mandy?"

Her head swam at the sight of him, standing tall and handsome in his black broadcloth suit. Mr. Henry's new secretary cowered at the sight of him.

His moustache and beard were newly trimmed, and his hat sat at just the right angle. What was he doing here, after the way she had treated him? How did he know that she needed him?

"Virgil, I—"

Virgil put an arm around her. "Mandy, you don't look spry." He glowered at the secretary. "Get up from there. Can't you see my wife don't feel well?"

The thin young man gave way, and Virgil seated her in his chair. "You need some air or something?"

"I just needed to sit down. My heart feels like it's going to leap out of my chest."

Now he glowered at her. "I knew you was coming back here. Don't know why, though."

She wiped her clammy palms on her black dress, leaving noticeable wet tracks.

The door to Charles Henry's office opened. Virgil turned and stood there to face her father's former partner, her husband as the very picture of Jovian displeasure.

Which made Charles Henry very red and very uncomfortable.

Amanda, instead of feeling nerves and gloom, felt a thrill climb from her toes to her fingertips. How effective Virgil was when he directed his ire at someone. And on her behalf.

Charles Henry struggled to keep calm. "What's going on out here?"

Amanda held onto the edge of the chair, finding the strength in her knees to stand. "This is my husband, Virgil Smithson."

Virgil stepped forward and stood over Charles Henry who had stuck out his hand. Virgil folded his arms to avoid contact. "I believe you has something to say to Mandy, and I hope you said it. I'm a man of God and don't believe in beating up on people, but I'ma make you sorry if you don't honor my Mandy like the lady she is."

CHAPTER TWENTY

Virgil nodded from a chair across from Charles Henry's desk. "So Mandy's daddy still owe you nine hundred dollars on her freedom papers when he die?"

"That's correct, Mr. Smithson. You seem to have a profound understanding of the situation."

Her husband shook his head. "I didn't know Realie, but of course Sally heard tell of her. Her big sister and all. They mammy have so many children, it wore her out. Sally and Isaac come last, but Realie was her first girl."

The tips of Amanda's fingers had ice in them. In August. She gripped the chair at all these revelations, not able to believe or understand. Why had her father not told her?

For protection, the same thing that Virgil had been talking about. It was better for her not to know. Her eyes smarted with tears, and Virgil covered her hand with his. Her fingers warmed under his touch, and he gave her hand a little squeeze.

"Amanda was just on her way to have a promissory note signed over by my secretary."

"Promissory note? What's that, saying she going to pay you?"

"Yes. Similar to the agreement that her father and I had. I drew off a certain portion of his pay every month."

No wonder they lived in boarding houses. She would often ask why they couldn't have a little house of their own, but he'd said that every single spare penny went to help free their enslaved brethren and that the least they could do by way of sacrifice was to live a little less well. The rest went to ensure they did live relatively well.

Now she understood. A stationary house, instead of moving around, would have made them more of a target for potential slave traders. A boardinghouse also offered cooked food and companionship, of a sort. Her father had tried so hard.

She whipped her hanky out of her pocket to apply to her watering eyes, painful with unshed tears.

"So you didn't live nice?"

"It was nice enough, Virgil. Papa believed in all of his money going to the cause. Now I understand why."

"Mr. Henry wants to transfer the note to you?"

"Yes. I suppose so."

Virgil's eyebrows came together in displeasure. "Without helping you to find a job of some kind?"

Oh, he'd offered her a job. Virgil glared at Charles Henry, and at least the man had the good grace to look ashamed.

Virgil stood and put his hands in his pockets. "Only one way to be rid of him."

Henry looked as if he were going to have an accident. The look on his face made laughter bubble up inside of her. She kept her face straight, though.

"How are you going to be rid of him?" she asked.

"I sign over the smithy to hold. It's worth that nine hundred now, if I were to sell it, but he can have thirty percent of what I make against it until it's paid off."

She shifted forward. "I won't let you do that, Virgil. No."

He sat down beside her once more, his hand on top of hers. "Mandy, it's done. This man's going to have the papers drawn up. You can look over them as you like, and I sign them like you taught me. You need to be free of him, and I'm helping you. Understand?"

Now her tears came. "I can't."

Virgil nodded and spoke to Charles Henry. "How long would it take to draw up the papers?"

"I can have those ready in an hour, Mr. Smithson. Thank you so much." He waddled out of the office, probably rubbing his hands together at getting a profitable blacksmith shop.

She turned to him. "Virgil, please, think about this. It's another kind of slavery. To him."

"We be fine. He'll be paid off in two years, I figure. I have my money from the town and from building houses. I'm rebuilding the schoolhouse, the church. Just as you want it, Mandy, 'cause you know best."

Sliding back in her seat, she had to reflect on the irony of it all. Who was the richer? She with no money and a fine education? Or her husband who had growing literacy skills, but could more than take care of himself and her?

Not unlike the first time she'd seen him, the smile on his face came bursting through his stern countenance and looked, as she'd understood it before, like the sun. "You feeling better?"

"Much." She slid forward and put both hands in his. "Virgil. Thank you so much."

"No, Mandy. You've brought so much more to me. Paying this man so he can leave you alone and stop you from feeling poorly about yourself—that's what matters."

She leaned forward, and he did too, more than halfway. Their knees met first, but once he moved his out of the way, they edged closer, smiling. Their lips met on target with no hesitation, regrets, or apologies.

When they parted, the declaration came from him first, straight from his heart. "I love you, Mrs. Smithson."

Her heart surged. "And I love you, Mr. Smithson."

He put his hand on her braids and traced them, staring at each one of them, then at her. "When we gets back to Milford, to our house, you coming in to my room. To stay."

She sneaked a look at the door, captured the hand touching her hair, and kissed his palm. "Yes, I will."

"Well. Do God."

"Yes."

For good measure, she leaned forward to kiss him again, because she liked it.

After a brief visit to her father's grave, Mandy insisted they take the night train home. "I spoke to some of the summer students about coming down until the term starts up in October, so Crumpton will have a teacher. But it's not home. Milford is." It was home in a number of ways she hadn't even realized.

She could have been March.

She could have been Sally.

So, her few things packed with all of the papers in his pocket, she and Virgil rode on the night train. For the entire trip, Virgil had his arms around her, which was a very nice feeling indeed. Her arrival in Milford was different this time with the midday sun shining down on them.

Hand in hand, they made their way up the slight rise that was now so familiar. Milford was her home. Virgil was her husband. March was her daughter. And she had uncles and aunts and cousins—she was part of a community now.

When they arrived at the smithy, Isaac came out to them, a concerned look on his face. "Glad you made it back. Mrs. Milford, she doing mighty poorly right about now. She keep asking for you, Virgil."

"Just got in on the train."

"Yeah, we was told to watch out for you. With Mandy next to you of course. Pauline say that."

"We can go home to get ready and—"

Isaac shook his head. Her uncle. "No time for that. You got to get up there. Leave the bag behind. I just finished shoeing this horse. She ready. Go on and take her."

Virgil guided the reins over the horse's head. He lifted Amanda as if she weighed nothing and set her on the horse. He rode astride in front of her. "Hold on," he said.

She wrapped her arms around his narrow waist and leaned into the broadcloth, burying her face in it, inhaling the comforting smell of him. She might have enjoyed this feeling if there hadn't been the shadow of Mrs. Milford hanging over them. What did she want?

The feel of Mandy's arms about him made Virgil sit straight up on the horse. He could ride on forever this way, but before he knew it, they eased up in front of the Milford house.

He helped Mandy down as the butler threw open the main door. "She been calling for you."

Charles's wrinkled features were arranged in true fear. Virgil's heart pounded just a bit extra. Maybe this really was it for Mrs. Milford. "We here. We'll go on up."

They went up the stairs and into Mrs. Milford's bedroom, where she lay on the bed, still and quiet with Dr. Mason from Crumpton attending to her.

"She had a good day yesterday," The flame-haired Dr. Mason pointed out to them. "Fast decline today. Don't know if she'll last the day."

"Virgil." Millicent Milford's voice called out, small and weak.

He stepped forward. "I'm here, ma'am."

Dr. Mason whispered, "Talk to her, but not for long. She needs to rest."

The doctor left the room but left the door open. What was that all about? They wasn't about to do her no harm.

"I'm glad you come. And you brought your wife with you."

"I did."

"I've got to say to you, before God Almighty calls me home, that I've long known we would pay for what we did in slavery. I'm paying now, dying in this awful pain. I'm just suffering so."

"Sorry to hear that, ma'am."

"I just want you to know I would have never sold Sally away if I had known what those people were going to do to her. I only knew what happened here at Milford, and Mr. Milford never sought to attack the female slaves."

"I see, ma'am."

The room quieted. Was he supposed to say more than that?

Small tears glinted in the corners of Mrs. Milford's eyes. "It's hard living in the country without help. I would have freed our slaves a long time ago, if Georgia law didn't say they had to leave if they were free. I couldn't run this place by myself. It's all just terribly mixed up. I'm glad it's over. I'm ready to face God's judgement."

Beside him, Amanda nodded. She moistened her lips in the silence, then spoke. "Do you recall a maid of yours named Aurelia or Realie?"

"Oh, yes. Realie was the maid assigned to me as a bride. I'd been an old maid when I married, but I still didn't know how life worked in the South."

"And she taught you."

"Oh my, yes. She was a very quick young woman. I was grateful for her when she came and then so sorry when she ran off. Mr. Milford looked all over for her, and then we got a notice from a lawyer who wanted to pay for her lost service. He wanted her back of course, but she'd gone up north and made a new life for herself. We took the money."

"She was my mother."

"Oh, my dear." Mrs. Milford wheezed a thin cough out from her lungs. "You don't much resemble her."

"I've been told I look more like my father."

"He came down to give us the money in exchange. I see it now, in your face. A little like an Indian. He had to wait for her to come back from when the slave catchers caught her. He refused to stay in our home."

" Did you know that she'd had a child? Me?"

Mrs. Milford's eyes went sightless.

"Ma'am?" Virgil said.

"I'm thinking, Virgil. I haven't gone to the Lord yet. Amanda, I don't remember. Mr. Milford probably knew."

"Is that why you wrote to my father to send a teacher? Because you saw him as a connection?"

"I just sent to the people Mr. Milford knew."

Mandy stood up. "My goodness."

"Seems as if you were destined to be here, dear. For Virgil. It does my heart good to see him happy before I leave this earth. I'm so sorry about what happened to Sally, but I'm glad you've come along to make him happy. Have you?"

Virgil set a hand on Mandy's waist. "She has. I love my wife."

"Praise God." The breath the old lady took in rattled into the quiet of the room. Then she said, "I wonder, Amanda. If you don't mind an old lady's request…"

"What is it, ma'am?"

The woman focused on Mandy. "Please read me some of the Bible. You offered before."

Mandy looked up at him. He knew what she was thinking as clearly as if she'd said it. That was before she knew that Mrs. Milford had been her mother's owner. A new view changed a lot of things.

But Mandy picked up the family Bible on the bedside stand. "We'll both read to you, if that's all right."

Mrs. Milford's eyes grew wide. "Virgil?"

"I'll pick it out. Might be a little slow, but I'll try."

"Good practice for you." Mandy offered him the Bible.

He nodded.

The hazel glints danced in Mandy's eyes. "I'll be here for you if you need help."

He knew she would be.

"Should we read anything in particular?" Mandy asked.

"No. Just start at Genesis."

Day passed into night and started into morning. Virgil had fallen asleep to the soothing sound of Mandy reading but jolted awake in his chair when she stopped. He took her into his arms as Dr. Mason examined Mrs. Milford. "She's not with us anymore."

Mrs. Milford's slack-jawed appearance more than confirmed it.

Rest in peace, ma'am.

"Let's go home, wife." They held each other as they went down the stairs and outside. He helped his wife up onto the horse.

"What about March?" Mandy asked his back as she snugly wrapped her arms around him.

"She's sleeping at her Pauline's, so I'm not waking her now. It's a perfect chance for us to... spend time together." He couldn't help the hoarseness in his voice. "That fine by you?"

"Yes. Can you go a little faster?"

He urged the horse on, more than willing to oblige her and make her happy. As he had promised.

In his capacity as mayor, Virgil called for two days of mourning for Mrs. Milford. The cotton crop was about to come in and, being the hottest part of summer, he didn't want to keep the body any longer than necessary.

He built the casket himself out of pure pine while Isaac went to Crumpton and told the important people there. He took Mandy with him to send telegrams to Mrs. Milford's daughters-in-law up north. They might not be able to make it in time for the funeral, but the family should know.

Given the August heat, Mrs. Milford was laid to rest the next day, next to her husband. The gate of iron erected around her husband's grave be extended to include her as well.

Mrs. Milford's lawyer called him into the parlor of the house after the services were over.

"I would have spoken to you about this when I was here the other day, but folks say you were gone."

"I was up north with my wife."

"Will you call her in as well? This concerns her."

He went outside where large planks and sawhorses had been set up to hold raisin cookies and lemonade. March rarely got lemonade and she danced around, begging for more. Virgil sure hoped his wife did not oblige their daughter. "Mandy, will you step in here please?"

Mandy wore her black, but today she'd put on a white collar and cuffs too. The lighter color made her look happier and showed off her dimples. The sight gladdened his heart considerably. What a beautiful sight she made.

"Yes, Virgil?"

He beckoned to her, and she joined him in the parlor. He had only been there once before, when Mr. Milford had given him his freedom papers. Otherwise, the door was always closed on the sad-looking room with compromised velvet drapes and cabbage-rose carpet worn out from Union troops dirtying up everything. The house was a for-sure mess from what it had been.

He sat on the davenport with Mandy, his hand on her waist and her hand in his. "How may we help you?" she asked.

"I'm the Milford attorney. Took over that position from my daddy when he died."

"I'm so sorry to hear that, sir." Mandy nodded in sympathy with the man. Virgil squeezed her waist a bit to support her.

"Mrs. Milford called me out here to make an amendment to her will, just the other day. It involves you."

"Us?"

"Yes." He waved a paper. "She left you and your wife, jointly, the house, the grounds, and the lands. Her family gets the money, a sum that doesn't amount to much in the wake of the war."

Mandy's hands shook. "May I see that?"

She held the paper straight. As she could.

Dear Virgil and Amanda,

You both have lightened the burden of these last days considerably. Given that my son's wives have not shown the least interest in this part of the country, they can have what's in the bank accounts. In perpetuity, you and your heirs shall be the holders of the grounds, lands, and house of the Milford farm. It would be my hope that, given the location of the house, it would be a compromise candidate for a school between Crumpton and Milford, but you chalk this up to the silly wish of an old woman. It's not giving you Sally back, but everything that was her is in this ramshackle house. Whatever you end up doing, I know it will be wise and will benefit your people who suffered under the terrible yoke of slavery for so long. God bless you both. Long life, health, and love to you.

Millicent V. Milford

"Maybe she knew about what happened at the school," Virgil mused.

"She knew. She wanted to help." His wife whipped out a hanky, and he patted her arm. She took a deep breath as she used the white hanky on her face. "One of my classmates is supposed to arrive next week to have a small summer session. Beyond that we will have to see."

"Yes. Well. Here it is." The lawyer gestured with lips pressed thin. "All yours."

"Does the coming crop belong to us or to the family?"

A good question, wife. Virgil eyed his woman with pride.

"It's part of the land as of now. It's yours."

She turned to him, and those hazel glints showed up again. "We can pay off Charles Henry."

"I don't know if we need to worry about that just now. We got time to think about it. Sure wasn't expecting her to do this."

The lawyer stood up to leave. "I have to warn you. Once Milford daughters find out, they won't be happy. The older one is the one with the two girls and she might file suit on their behalf. I would if I were her."

The mean look in the lawyer's eyes made Virgil know what he was going to do as soon as he left here, if he hadn't already. He would make sure Clara and Lucy found out about how their mother-in-law skipped over them. So be it. Sally's bones, blood and tears were in this house. He wasn't giving it up without a fight.

After he left, Virgil and Mandy embraced and kissed for a long time.

Virgil spoke after they'd pulled apart for air. "What we going to do, wife?"

"I think we should offer to help build the school in Crumpton and use the house to get the Milford school going again. We can build a normal school here on Milford land to train people with enough knowledge how to teach. Then we don't have to send so far for teachers anymore."

"I think that's a fine idea. We call it after her. Milford College."

"Yes. This way there won't need to be so much competition, noise, threats, or whatever. Everyone can help."

He put his hand on the small of her back and guided her out of their parlor. While it was great to celebrate the Lord's bounty, it was best not to gloat over it. They stood on the porch, hand in hand, watching March get more lemonade for herself, enjoying the company of those with them presently. The Baxters. Amanda's family.

What would the future look like? What responsibilities would they have?

The weight, the heavy weight he hadn't even known he carried, lifted from his heart. God blessed him and removed the heavy weight. For the first time in a long while, he knew God was pleased with him. He knew he had kept his promise to the ones who'd gone on to glory before them. His hand relaxed in hers.

He had more than paid and was free. Amanda was free too, and as he squeezed his wife's delicate hand, he was joyous that their liberty made them free to love each other. Whatever came their way, they would face it strong—together forever in God's love.

Author's Note

Fiction is written about exceptional people. Reconstruction Era Georgia was made up of exceptional people who cherished dreams showing how a people can be made free through their studies. Mary Peake, like Amanda, went elsewhere to help the enslaved learn how to read and write. She began her quest before the Civil War ended. She died young and early in her journey, but many others of all races took up her cause and went to the southern states to establish schools of education to teach an people.

William Gold(ing) was an illiterate former minister who established a school in Liberty County and hired Eliza Davis to come and teach the formerly enslaved how to read and write. Other places and towns in the south, like Mount Blanc in Mississippi saw racial cooperation and the establishment of communities in the hopes that people could learn, over time, how to live side by side in peace.

Others had different ideas. Our conceptions of this time period were written into history by those who were ultimately victorious over these potential office holders and educators. Still, the exceptional people harbored a dream that grew within them over time. *The Mayor's Mission* will tell more about how that dream carried on through hard times for the Smithson family.…

Coming Autumn 2014: *The Mayor's Mission*

2 Corinthians 6:14 - Be ye not unequally yoked together with unbelievers: for what fellowship hath righteousness with unrighteousness? and what communion hath light with darkness?

Is it possible for a newly formed family to hold onto all they have during the swiftly moving tides of change in Reconstruction Era Georgia? Will they be able to hold onto each other? God tests the newly formed bond of Virgil and Amanda to ensure their resolve to build Milford College holds firm…..

Milford, GA 1868:

Mayor Virgil Smithson has been away at the constitutional convention in the newly established state capitol in Atlanta for almost five months. He's late in getting back home. Meanwhile, Amanda Smithson manages the crowded and growing Milford College by herself. How they will pay the taxes on the school property if Virgil doesn't return from Atlanta?

The problems pile up. The Milford daughters-in-law arrive, determined to wrest what they see as their rightful inheritance from the Smithsons. Amanda has hired an old school chum from Oberlin to teach the older students who is a tad too affectionate with Amanda for Virgil's liking. And, just when it all seems impossible to resolve, the Smithsons must endure another crisis that threatens to tear them, and the school apart forever.

When life becomes difficult, it will take all of God's love and mercy for the Smithsons to come back together within the bonds of holy matrimony that united them less than two years before. It will be the mission of the mayor and his wife to fight for the existence of the coltish educational tradition that they established together. And to keep their love alive.

ABOUT THE AUTHOR

Piper G Huguley is the author of the "Home to Milford College" series. The series traces the love stories at a small "Teachers and Preachers" college in Georgia over time, beginning with the love story of the founders. Book one in the series, *The Preacher's Promise*, was a semi-finalist in Harlequin's So You Think You Can Write contest, and a quarter-finalist in the 2014 Amazon Breakthrough Novel Award contest. The prequel novella, *The Lawyer's Luck*, and *The Preacher's Promise* will be independently published in July 2014. *The Mayor's Mission* will be independently published in the fall of 2014.

Huguley is also the author of "Migrations of the Heart," a five-book series of inspirational historical romances set in the early 20th century featuring African American characters. Book one in the series, *A Virtuous Ruby* won the Golden Rose contest in Historical Romance in 2013 and is a Golden Heart finalist in 2014. Book four in the series, *A Champion's Heart*, was a Golden Heart finalist in 2013.

Piper Huguley blogs about the history behind her novels at piperhuguley.com. She lives in Atlanta, Georgia with her husband and son.

Books by Piper Huguley

The Lawyer's Luck

The love story of Amanda Smithson's parents

Available in print and on Kindle, Nook, Kobo and iTunes.

97641712R00146

Made in the USA
Columbia, SC
18 June 2018